CHINOOK MIDDLE SCHOOL LIBRARY

P9-DDG-198

00934 5820

DATE DUE

NOV 1 7 2015	MAY 0 9 2019	
OCT 1 0 2016		
MAR 2 4 2017		
NOV 1 7 2017		
FEB 0 8 2018		
APR 0 6 2018		
DEC 0 5 2018		
JAN 0 7 2018		
GAYLORD		PRINTED IN U.S.A.

NOV 1 2 2015

CHINOOK MIDDLE SCHOOL
LIBRARY

Also by
Royce Buckingham:

Demonkeeper

GOBLINS!
AN UnderEarth Adventure

By Royce Buckingham

G. P. Putnam's Sons

G. P. PUTNAM'S SONS

A division of Penguin Young Readers Group.

Published by The Penguin Group.

Penguin Group (USA) Inc., 375 Hudson Street, New York, NY 10014, U.S.A.

Penguin Group (Canada), 90 Eglinton Avenue East, Suite 700, Toronto, Ontario M4P

2Y3, Canada (a division of Pearson Penguin Canada Inc.).

Penguin Books Ltd, 80 Strand, London WC2R 0RL, England.

Penguin Ireland, 25 St. Stephen's Green, Dublin 2, Ireland

(a division of Penguin Books Ltd.).

Penguin Group (Australia), 250 Camberwell Road, Camberwell, Victoria 3124, Australia

(a division of Pearson Australia Group Pty Ltd).

Penguin Books India Pvt Ltd, 11 Community Centre, Panchsheel Park,

New Delhi - 110 017, India.

Penguin Group (NZ), 67 Apollo Drive, Rosedale, North Shore 0632, New Zealand

(a division of Pearson New Zealand Ltd).

Penguin Books (South Africa) (Pty) Ltd, 24 Sturdee Avenue, Rosebank,

Johannesburg 2196, South Africa.

Penguin Books Ltd, Registered Offices: 80 Strand, London WC2R 0RL, England.

Copyright © 2008 by Royce Buckingham. All rights reserved.

This book, or parts thereof, may not be reproduced in any form

without permission in writing from the publisher, G. P. Putnam's Sons,

a division of Penguin Young Readers Group, 345 Hudson Street, New York, NY 10014.

G. P. Putnam's Sons, Reg. U.S. Pat. & Tm. Off. The scanning, uploading and

distribution of this book via the Internet or via any other means without the permission

of the publisher is illegal and punishable by law. Please purchase only authorized

electronic editions, and do not participate in or encourage electronic piracy of

copyrighted materials. Your support of the author's rights is appreciated.

The publisher does not have any control over and does not assume any

responsibility for author or third-party websites or their content.

Published simultaneously in Canada. Printed in the United States of America.

Design by Marikka Tamura. Text set in MrsEaves.

Library of Congress Cataloging-in-Publication Data

Buckingham, Royce.

Goblins! : an UnderEarth adventure / by Royce Buckingham. p. cm.

Summary: Twelve-year-old Sam Hill and seventeen-year-old PJ discover a scary world

of goblins under the earth after one of the creatures escapes through a tunnel in the

ground, and when Sam follows it back down, PJ must go underground to rescue him.

[1. Goblins—Fiction. 2. Adventure and adventurers—Fiction.

3. Fathers and sons—Fiction. 4. Washington (State)—Fiction.] I. Title.

PZ7.B879857Go 2008   [Fic]—dc22   2008001146

ISBN 978-0-399-25002-6

1 3 5 7 9 10 8 6 4 2

This book is dedicated to:

My friends Mike and Eric,
who were once twelve years old with me and, in my heart, still are.

My benefactors at AEI,
Ken Atchity, Chi-Li Wong, and Michael Kuciak, who believed in me.

My hardworking and infinitely reasonable editor,
John Rudolph at Putnam.

And always my wonderful parents,
my amazing wife, and my boys.

BOSTON

PROLOGUE

The young guardian's snores echoed across the vast, dim cavern below him. His leather armor hung loose around his chest, and his sword lay neglected across his lap. With his eyes open, he could have seen for a mile across the shadowy plains of UnderEarth. But the towering subterranean fortress wall built into the sheer rock cliff had not been so much as spat upon by an enemy in more than a year, and so there seemed no reason to keep his eyes open.

Twang-ang-ang!

He woke slowly and stared in sleepy wonder at a crooked shaft vibrating in the wall just above his head. *How strange*, he thought. Then he realized it was an arrow. He gasped and leapt for the huge warning bell a short distance away. A thick layer of dust covered the bell's ancient stone surface, which hadn't been touched for many months. It could save him now, though, he hoped. The bell hung ready, promising to alert the rest of the soldiers and bring help, but as he ran toward it, more crooked arrows pelted the wall in his path.

Whap! Whap! Whap!

An arrow glanced off his helmet, and another zipped

past his nose, so close to him that he could hear it slice the air. He scrambled back the way he'd come and ducked behind a battlement, not daring to stick his head out again.

A primitive grappling hook flew over the wall and landed beside him, trailed by an attached rope. The hook lodged in the wall and the rope went taut. The guardian couldn't leave his shelter to dislodge it. Instead, he stretched his arm out and tilted a dark, steaming cauldron toward the wall. Boiling oil poured over the edge, and an inhuman yelp exploded from the other side, then fell away.

He glanced about, wide-eyed. There was no other route off the wall. He tried for the bell again, but another hail of wobbly arrows kept him from it. His cauldron was empty. More hooks cleared the battlements, landing all around him. They were coming.

The young guardian closed his eyes again, hoping for a moment it was all a nightmare. Then a large, furry paw reached over the battlement and its powerful grip closed on his neck, and he knew for certain it was not just a bad dream. Unable to reach the bell, he could only shout a last, desperate warning to his unsuspecting friends on the other side of the wall. But just as he opened his mouth, the furry arm hauled him off his feet and over the edge, and his cry faded unheard into the cavern below.

"Gobliiiiiins!"

1
SAM

One hundred feet directly above the fortress wall, on the surface of the earth, Sam Hill loitered on the curb outside the Stop-n-Sip contemplating the most potentially exciting thing to happen in his tiny hometown of Sumas, Washington, in the entire month of June. A white truck with the words DRAGON'S BREATH FIREWORKS stenciled in flaming orange and red on its side turned into the parking lot and rolled to a stop at the gas pump.

Sam trailed the driver, who ambled inside to pay for gas. The driver selected a beef stick from the aging collection in the plastic bin on the counter and grabbed a ZOWIE! soda. He came out holding the life-sized welded metal salmon sculpture, to which was attached the station's tiny bathroom key. He headed to the restroom out back, leaving his truck unguarded and unlocked.

At twelve years old, Sam was old enough to know better than to do what he was about to do, but the truck was not carrying ordinary little sparklers and smoke bombs. Dragon's Breath made big, industrial-strength fireworks for town displays on the Fourth of July. Years ago, when his mom was still around, Sam had gone with his parents into Bellingham to see one of the big shows. The huge fireworks had lit up the entire night in a rainbow of colors. He'd watched in wonder as tiny points of light arced high into the darkness, where they burst with ear-pounding explosions into gigantic blooming flowers of fire and burning rain that fell from the sky. *Nothing like that ever happens in Sumas,* Sam thought.

As far as Sam was concerned, living in Sumas was like growing up in a rural coma. The town was nestled in the foothill forests of the Cascade mountain range. Its main street was just a one-block strip of mom-and-pop shops, the Stop-n-Sip, and a mercantile. The town wasn't big enough for a Wal-Mart or even a McDonald's—*no real civilization of any kind.* He frowned.

Now that school was out, Sam was free to do whatever he wanted until his dad wandered home from the tavern, but he was bored with daytime TV, hanging out at the gas station had quickly gotten old, and he'd explored the woods so many times that he knew all the trails around Sumas by heart. He wasn't old enough to drive, so he couldn't even head into Bellingham for a movie, unless, of course, he "borrowed" a car. He'd snuck off with his dad's old truck before, but he wasn't tall enough to see over the dashboard very well, so he never went very far.

A kid had to make his own fun in Sumas, Sam thought, like the time he'd created a make-believe ocean in back of the church with a garden hose—except that he'd made it a little too close to the church basement and the pastor had discovered his couches floating downstairs. There was also the time he'd pretended that passing 18-wheelers were

GOBLINS!

enemy tanks and ambushed them, launching mortar shells freshly picked from Mr. Richey's tomato garden. He'd gotten in trouble for that too.

Sam eyed the multicolored painting of exploding fireworks on the unlocked truck door. *Setting off a couple of those in the woods would be an adventure,* he thought. He glanced at the bathroom door. It was still closed.

Sam dashed to the door and quickly wedged a rock beneath it to block it shut. He slipped around to the front of the station and checked to make sure the attendant wasn't watching, then he ran across the parking lot, climbed into the cab of the truck, and slid into the rear compartment. He threw back the canvas that covered the truck's cargo and gasped. The bed of the truck was full of boxes brimming with fireworks, hundreds of them. *They'll never miss one or two,* Sam thought. *How could I possibly get into trouble?*

2
PJ

As Sam Hill rummaged in the fireworks truck, PJ Myrmidon rumbled toward Sumas through the tranquil Washington woods in his snorting, olive green '69 Camaro. He wiped grime off of the inside of his windshield and spotted a sign that read:

SUMAS, WASHINGTON—10 MILES
CANADA—11 MILES

Ten more minutes of freedom, he thought. After three days on the road, he was almost at the end of his trip. He fed the growling Camaro more gas, tapped the steering wheel, and whipped his long hair to a thumping song by the group Slug Bait. Other rock band stickers littered his bumper— Social Disease, Shelf Life, The Wags—and his California license plate rattled in its frame. Fast-food wrappers and soda cans were stacked shin-high on the floorboards. PJ reached down into the pile and fished out a half-eaten burger. It was soggy, mushed, and a couple days old. "Sweet!" PJ grinned, and he raised it to his mouth.

Ten miles later, PJ roared into Sumas. It was evening, the sun was dipping behind the fir trees, and not a single business was open. It wasn't even dark yet, but humans were nowhere to be seen. An old dog slumped in a doorway of one of the little shops, but it lay so still that PJ wasn't sure it was alive. The entire tiny town seemed dead, especially for a kid from L.A.

Just then, flashing blue and red lights appeared behind him. PJ groaned and eased off the gas. His tires crunched gravel on the side of the road and he coasted to a stop, cranking the Camaro's old broken handle to lower his window. The rich, green smell of farms and forest flooded into the car, and PJ could hear birds chirping at each other as though having a friendly argument.

The police officer approached, glanced at his license plate, and leaned down beside the car to frown in at him through the window. "Going a little fast there, weren't you, son?"

"Sorry," PJ said lamely.

"And what on earth are you doing driving all the way up here from California by yourself?"

"What?" PJ shrugged. "I'm seventeen."

"Exactly my point. You're *only* seventeen."

"Driving isn't a crime. I got my license now. See?" PJ held out his license.

The officer took it and examined the photo. "Having a license is a privilege. Don't abuse it by speeding in my town, Percy."

PJ winced. "I go by PJ now."

"Well, you're late, PJ."

"Only by a day."

"Just meet me over at the station, son. And drive slow, eh?"

"Yes, Officer," PJ said, rolling his eyes. "And, hey, can I have my license back . . . Dad?"

Officer Myrmidon handed the license back to his son, turned away, and strode to the police cruiser. PJ put the Camaro in gear and followed the patrol car down the road to Sumas's modest police station. The cruiser rolled behind the small, official-looking building, while PJ and the Camaro rattled to a stop out front.

PJ shook his head. His father had never left the small town where he had gotten his first job as a volunteer police officer over twenty years earlier. PJ was used to leaving, though. He and his mother had left this town for California when he was a boy, and after he'd turned sixteen and gotten his license, he began to leave his mom's house whenever he felt like it too.

He climbed out, stretching his stiff limbs. A small, wooden sign rose from the lawn in front of him:

COMMITMENT, SECURITY, RESPONSIBILITY
JOHN H. MYRMIDON
OFFICER IN RESIDENCE

PJ looked down at his T-shirt, which had an anarchy symbol emblazoned on the front. "Maybe I'm adopted," he muttered, and he headed up the walk, wondering vaguely who the little freckle-faced kid was he'd seen sitting in the back of his dad's patrol car.

GOBLINS!

3
SAM AND PJ

Sam sat in the Sumas police station's only jail cell. He had felt guilty about leaving the driver trapped in the bathroom. The Stop-n-Sip toilet was, as far as Sam could tell, the stinkiest place in Sumas. Before making his getaway, he ran past the door and kicked the rock loose, then he ducked behind the station billboard with his loot. The driver had emerged, puzzled, then shrugged and got into his truck, no doubt moving on to bigger, more exciting places, and he pulled away, none the wiser.

Just as Sam stepped out from behind the billboard, a hand fell on his shoulder. It was Officer Myrmidon. Sam usually liked seeing the town's only policeman—Officer Myrmidon had watched out for Sam after his mom left, giving Sam unclaimed coats, sneakers, and toys from the lost and found at the police station. And he always took the time to talk to Sam when he saw him.

Sam knew he couldn't deceive Officer Myrmidon, so when the policeman had asked, "Hey, Sam, what are you hauling there?" and pointed to his bulging backpack, Sam had simply sighed, handed over the pack, and climbed into the rear seat of the police car without making a fuss. He knew the drill—he'd been in the backseat of the police car before.

On the way to the station, they'd pulled over a kid in a vintage Camaro. It was funny, Sam thought, because the kid turned out to be Officer Myrmidon's son. He was an older kid with long hair, not at all what Sam would have pictured, and they didn't seem particularly friendly with each other.

When they arrived at the station, Officer Myrmidon dumped the stolen fireworks into the garbage, tossed the empty pack on his desk, and ushered Sam into the one-room police station's jail cell.

"Okay, you're in here until your dad comes to pick you up," the tall policeman said. "Remember, this was a choice. Your decisions out there determine whether you wind up in here."

The door clanged shut, and he was behind bars. It was a bright spring-almost-summer day, and instead of enjoying the smells of the fresh spring grass, new flowers, and burnt fireworks, he was in jail. Sam sighed loudly. *Not much of an adventure*, he thought.

Sam slumped on the cell bench in his baggy cargo pants and a black concert T-shirt for the band Lobotomy. The cell was bare except for a toilet and some toys Officer Myrmidon had tossed in with him to help him pass the time—a foam bat, a ball, and a deck of cards. The place smelled sterile. Sam played poker against himself beside the metal toilet and tapped the foam bat against the wall. He pretended to ignore the tension between the older kid and his cop dad across the room but secretly kept one ear tuned in.

"I wish you'd been on time for once," Officer Myrmidon said to PJ. "I had thought we might go fishing . . . yesterday."

"Fish should still be there, right?" PJ said.

"I have responsibilities today. You familiar with those?"

"Like paying your bills, doing your laundry, sticking with your wife? Stuff like that?"

Officer Myrmidon looked up, hurt. "How is your mother?"

PJ took a seat in the interrogation chair. "She's fine. Happy, I think. She's dating now."

Sam saw PJ's dad wince.

The big officer sat at his small oak desk and glanced at his computer screen. He typed quickly, then rose and grabbed his coat. "I just got confirmation that some climbers are missing in caves south of here. I need to take the truck to help with search and rescue. Wait here until I get back. Call my cell if anything comes up, anything at all."

"You're leaving?" PJ said. "But I just got here."

"I took *yesterday* off," his dad said, "the day you were supposed to be here. I have local duties today and a border to guard."

"You're not with the federal border patrol," PJ said. "You're just a small-town cop."

"There's no one else for hundreds of miles out here. Who do you think is keeping us safe?"

"From what? Drunk Canadians?"

"I need to go," his dad said.

"This sucks," PJ said. "More than usual."

"I'm sorry we can't be together right now, but my job is important."

"Huh. That sounds familiar." PJ frowned.

"Just wait here," his dad said. "Our young guest's father should be coming soon. The key is on the desk. But don't let him take Sam in his car if he's . . ." Officer Myrmidon made a bottle-tipping motion with his hand, then went to the door. "If that happens, tell him you don't have the key and he'll have to wait until I get back."

"Aye-aye, sir. Any other responsibilities you want to lay on me while you're gone? Finish school? Find a job? Make something of myself?" PJ grabbed a police baton and rattled the bars of the cell, causing Sam to misshuffle and scatter his cards. "Feed the monkey?"

PJ's dad appeared at his son's shoulder like silent lightning. He grabbed the baton, twisted it away from PJ, and whirled it under his own arm in one smooth motion. PJ stared, surprised. "Don't do anything," his father said, placing the baton on the desk and walking back to the door. "That's what everyone's come to expect from you, right?" Then Officer Myrmidon slipped out like a whisper.

Sam gathered up his cards and snuck the deck into one of the many pockets of his oversized cargo pants alongside a butane cigarette lighter he wasn't supposed to have.

PJ slumped in his dad's chair and put his feet up. He pushed off and spun in a circle, tapping the baton in his hand and glancing at Sam. "Hey, little dude, when's your dad gonna be here to get you?"

"He should be here as soon as happy hour is over."

GOBLINS!

"Quality family life, I see."

"Like you," Sam shot back.

"Take a long walk off a short dock, convict."

"I'm not convicted yet," Sam said, "on this new charge."

"Oh, yeah? What're you in for?" PJ asked as he rifled through his father's desk drawer.

"Illegal fireworks."

"My dad put you in the slam for a few firecrackers? Man, he *is* uptight."

"They were the big ones, and some of 'em sorta ended up in my backpack." Sam pointed through the bars at the garbage.

PJ looked at the trash. "Whew! Nice. I oughtta find a way to dispose of these myself." PJ began to pull the fireworks from the can and stuff them back into Sam's pack. "By the way, something tells me this isn't your first time in the pokey, am I right?"

Sam hung his head. "No, but it's the last time. Your dad says that next fall he's gonna help me get back into the school that kicked me out and get a job when I'm old enough."

"Made you some promises, did he?" PJ smirked.

"I'm gonna change everything around," Sam proclaimed.

"Hate to be the bearer of bad news, little fella, but people don't change, not really. You got a criminal record at twelve, and the most likely job in your future is to hold up the Stop-n-Sip someday."

"Where you'll be working," Sam snapped back.

"Leave me alone," PJ said. "I'm a busy man." He resumed spinning in the chair.

BEEP-BEEP-BEEP! An alarm shrieked, and PJ fell out of his chair. He floundered up wide-eyed, holding the nightstick out in front of him like a cross against evil.

"Hey, delinquent, what's that beeping?" he said.

"A border sensor," Sam said.

"A what?"

"A police motion detector at the U.S.–Canadian border. I heard your dad once tell a guy on the phone that it goes off when smugglers sneak across and drop off bags of stuff in the woods."

"What kind of stuff?" PJ said, growing interested.

"Things they don't want to take through customs in their car—illegal contraband, tax-free cigarettes . . . bundles of cash in small denominations."

PJ's eyebrows shot up, and Sam hoped PJ wasn't thinking what he thought PJ was thinking. He'd already gotten into enough trouble for one day.

GOBLINS!

4
SMUGGLERS

PJ drove his father's patrol car. His dad had taken the police truck and left the cruiser behind with the key under the visor. The sun was setting, and Sam sat in the back of the car behind the safety cage.

"So let me get this straight, freckles," PJ said to Sam. "Smugglers walk across the Canadian border and drop bags of cash by a road on this side . . . ?"

Sam nodded. "Then they walk back into Canada, drive to the checkpoint, and come into the U.S. legally with nothing in their car for customs to find."

PJ grinned. "Then they zip down the road here on the U.S. side and pick it up. Briiiiiilliant!"

"If your dad catches us, I'm telling him you forced me to come," Sam said, "*and* that you have my fireworks."

"Calm down," PJ boomed into the car's intercom. "I didn't exactly twist your arm. Besides, it's only ten minutes to the sensor, right? We grab the stuff. Ten minutes back. And . . . boom! We're in the green. If the smugglers come, they see this cop car and bolt. Worst case, if Dad's standing in the parking lot with that 'what are you punks up to?' look on his face when we get back, we smile, hand over the seized loot, and tell him we heard the alarm and just did his job for him. He gets the credit for the bust and thinks we're super-duper junior crime fighters. Briiilliant!"

Sam resigned himself to navigating for PJ from the backseat as they drifted along Sumas's narrow two-lane county roads in Officer Myrmidon's patrol car. Twilit farmland turned quickly to shadowy forest, and Sam directed PJ onto a gravel drive, then a dirt road, then a couple of ruts in the mud that were little more than a path. The trees grew closer, the underbrush grew thicker, and PJ eased his father's cruiser deep into the woods.

"There's the sensor," Sam said finally, pointing to a semicamouflaged post in the ground. "I found it exploring when I was running through here once."

"Running from who?" PJ smirked.

"No comment."

PJ turned the car's lights out, and the woods around them went dark. "Now we get out to look for the loot, right?" PJ said. He stopped the car and idled in place.

"What if the smugglers are around?" Sam blinked, peering into darkness.

PJ put on one of his father's spare POLICE jackets. "C'mon, we're already here. Besides, you said it takes an hour round trip to get to the border crossing and back. Any smugglers would probably still be forty minutes away."

PJ was reaching to put the car into park when something moved in the darkness. A patch of shadow shifted against a background of dark trees. As soon as he noticed it, it was gone. "What was that?" he said.

GOBLINS!

"What was what?" Sam said, staring into the forest. "I can't see a thing. It's pitch-black."

PJ reached down and flipped the headlight switch. The sudden light glared on a dark, husky human shape in front of the car. It waved a club-shaped object and brought it down onto the metal hood of the cruiser.

Wham!

"Smuggler!" Sam yelled.

PJ's foot was still on the gas pedal. He jammed it down instinctively, and the car lurched forward. There was no time for the figure to move. *Thud!* It went down like a bowling pin and disappeared beneath the bumper.

PJ hit the brakes and the police cruiser jerked to a stop. He took a deep breath and quickly locked the door.

"You hit him!" Sam cried.

"I know," PJ breathed, staring into the woods.

"He's under the car!"

"I know!"

"What if he's a farmer or something?" Sam said.

"You're the one who screamed that he was a smuggler."

"How do I know who he is?"

"It's your stupid little town!" PJ snapped.

A low, pained growl rose from beneath the car.

"He's alive," PJ said, relieved. "Let's get out of here."

"We can't leave him," Sam said. "There's no way he can be okay after you smushed him."

PJ shook his head. "Dude, I just ran over a guy in a borrowed police car. My instincts tell me to drive far away and never speak of this again."

"Hit and run? They take your license away for that if they catch you."

"What if he *is* a smuggler?" PJ protested.

"What if he isn't?"

Moments later, Sam and a reluctant PJ were crouching on their hands and knees trying to haul the dazed form out from the shadows under the car.

"I found his arms," PJ said, slapping his dad's police handcuffs onto a pair of very thick, hairy wrists in the darkness. "Feels like the dude's wearing gloves. Help me get him into the backseat."

Sam helped PJ pull, and, with a huge tug, the dark shape slid completely out from under the car. It was heavy and limp, but Sam could hear its uneven panting. They wouldn't be able to see any injuries, though, until they got it up under the dome light in the backseat.

"He's heavy," Sam reported, wrestling the lower torso of the slack body up off the ground.

PJ took hold of the arms he'd cuffed together in front of its body and heaved the figure up into the backseat. It was just over five feet tall, incredibly heavy, and smelled vaguely of dirt. Suddenly, it snorted like a pig and began to raise its arms. PJ yelped and put his shoulder against it. Sam jumped in to help, grabbing a leg. Together they shoved the entire thing into the car, then PJ slammed the door shut. "There!"

"Am I nuts," Sam said, panting, "or was that guy wearing a fur coat?"

"Don't know," PJ said. "I was too busy trying not to let

him kill us with this." PJ held up the spiked club that had fallen on the ground. It was a primitive weapon, like a medieval mace. It seemed to be made of hard stone, yet it weighed no more than a couple of pounds, and it had nasty barbs all over it. Both boys stared at the club, then looked in the window.

"A weapon," Sam said. "So he *is* a smuggler."

"What kind of smuggler carries a spiked club?" PJ said.

"A fat, hairy one?" Sam shrugged, and he tapped on the window like a kid peering into a fishbowl.

Suddenly, the figure rose up in the backseat and threw its palms against the window. Thick, black fur covered its entire body—it was not wearing a fur coat. Its hands were leathery, like those of a gorilla, and its fingers were tipped with long, yellow claws. It pushed its face up against the glass and stared back at Sam and PJ with huge yellow eyes. Two long tusks jutted up from its lower jaw. It was definitely not human.

Sam and PJ leapt back. They stood silent for a time as the thing blinked its saucer eyes and glowered at them. Neither could think of a single thing to say. Finally, the boys turned to each other.

"Now what?" PJ asked.

"We can't let it out here in the woods," Sam said, pointing nervously at its long claws. "What if it comes after us?"

"If we can't let it out, and we don't want to sit out here alone with it in the dark, then what do you suggest we do?"

Minutes later, the police car eased along the dirt road, out of the woods, and back toward the police station, with both boys in the front and their strange, furry passenger behind the safety cage in the rear.

Behind them in the woods, a three-foot-wide square of grass beside the sensor post shifted, then tilted upward on a hinge—a trapdoor in the forest floor. Beneath it, two sets of human eyes peered out after the receding vehicle's taillights.

5
CITIZEN'S ARREST

Sam stared back through the metal grate from the passenger seat of the police cruiser. The creature sat stroking its wiry fur with its cuffed hands, brooding. It had a powerful chest, long arms, and bowed legs, so its body looked vaguely like that of a great ape. But the long claws that jutted from its nimble fingers were larger than any ape's, and its eyes were like nothing Sam had ever seen—they were huge, yellow, and curious . . . *scheming*. Its blunt snout and the curved warthog tusks that protruded from its oversized mouth gave it a fearsome appearance, but it had long, pointed ears that stuck up like those of an Egyptian cat. They turned back and forth, alert, as though listening carefully, and they made the thing seem slightly less brutish somehow.

Sam and PJ pulled into the tiny police station parking lot.

"Okay, here we are," PJ said. "Now what's the next phase of your clever plan?"

Sam pulled a long, pointed instrument out from under the seat.

"What's that?" PJ asked.

"Taser," Sam replied. "Your dad told me he zaps bad

guys with it, and it incapacitates them up to a full minute."

"You want to zap a ferocious animal with a device designed to work on humans and drag it inside in less than one minute? That's your plan?"

"Unless you've got a better one."

PJ frowned for a moment, then snatched the Taser from Sam and stuck it through a hole in the safety cage.

BZZZZZZT!

The creature contorted and went limp. "Go!" PJ yelled.

The boys jumped out and hauled the beast from the back of the car, grunting and cursing at each other as they struggled to drag it across the sidewalk. The creature's head bumped up the steps as Sam fumbled the front door open. *Thump-bump-thump-bump.*

Once inside, they pushed, pulled, and rolled the thing across the floor toward the jail cell as fast as they could. Sam gave a heave, PJ gave a shove, and it flopped inside. PJ slammed the barred door closed with a *clang* just as the creature blinked awake.

It rose slowly and snuffled about the jail cell, shading its eyes from the artificial lights of the room. Its clawed hands flexed angrily. The boys could see now that a thick leather jerkin hung over its vital areas, like armor from the Dark Ages.

"What is it?" Sam asked, staring in wonder at the creature and its outfit. It sat on the bench with its head slumped into its deep chest, but Sam could still see its toothy ex-

GOBLINS!

pression. Its eyes darted about beneath its thick brows so that it looked like it was evaluating its surroundings.

"A deformed bear?" PJ suggested. The creature looked up, frowning. It spotted the foam toy bat in the cell and grabbed it, feeling its weight.

"No," Sam said, "it's more like a mutated monkey—it almost seems like it's thinking." He looked around and found the foam ball, which had rolled out of the cell. He tossed the ball back into the cell.

"Oh, yeah?" PJ said. He motioned for the beast to throw the ball back. To their surprise, the creature stooped and picked it up, then rolled it to the bars of the cell, within PJ's reach. "Hey, I think it understands," PJ said. He stepped forward and leaned down to grab the ball.

"Argh!" the creature growled. It leapt at PJ and slammed the bat against his head through the bars.

Wham-wham-wham!

"Ahhh!" PJ cried out as the thing beat him about the face and ears. Sam yanked PJ away as the creature continued to pummel him with the foam toy. They tumbled into a pile against the desk. PJ shook Sam off angrily, staring up at the beast in the cell. "You ungrateful, treacherous piece of . . . why'd you do that?"

"You're gonna call your dad now, aren't you?" Sam suggested.

"Oh, now there's a fine idea," PJ panted, hauling himself up. "What kind of crook are you? You don't call the adult you're going to get into the *most* trouble with."

GOBLINS! 23

"Well, it's not like you can just call animal control and have them come haul it away. . . ."

Moments later, PJ was at his father's desk with the phone book open, dialing the telephone. "Hi, animal control . . . ?"

PJ listened for several seconds, then recited the station address and hung up.

"The answering machine said they respond to after-hours messages within sixty minutes," PJ told Sam. "With any luck, my dad won't be back for seventy."

Just then, the front door swung open.

6
ANIMAL CONTROL

PJ and Sam stood up, each expecting his own father to walk through the door. Instead, two pale figures in long, dusty cloaks stepped inside—a young woman and an albino man. The pair tugged back their hoods and squinted in the light of the room. Their cloaks were slate gray and covered their entire bodies except for the primitive boots on their feet.

If they stood against a stone wall, Sam thought, *they would blend right in.*

The albino man was perhaps twenty years old. His skin, hair, and eyebrows were white, almost translucent. Even his pupils seemed colorless.

The woman was slightly younger, seventeen or eighteen—about PJ's age, Sam guessed. Her black hair was bound by a thick metal ring at the back of her head and shot straight down her neck until it disappeared into her robe. In contrast, her complexion was nearly white and smooth as milk. Her lips were light colored too, almost imperceptible against her skin, yet in the middle of her pale face sparkled two alert green eyes.

"Let me guess," PJ said, "animal control?"

The pair looked at each other. The man motioned for the woman to remain silent and spoke with an accent that sounded vaguely Canadian. "We are indeed here for the . . . animal."

Sam whispered to PJ, "Dogcatchers usually wear white coveralls, not gray robes."

"I don't care," PJ said, "as long as they get this thing out of here."

"Are you expecting anyone else?" the man said.

"Man, I hope not," PJ said. "Come on, it's back here."

The man and the woman followed PJ. Sam tried to get PJ's attention. "They're early too," he said.

"So I'll give them a break on their low-budget uniforms for being prompt," PJ said. "Now, shut up, if you please, and let me get us out of this mess." He walked the man and woman to the cell.

When the furry creature caught sight of the robed strangers, it began to hop around the cell. It tore at the bars on the window and pounded the walls as though desperately trying to escape.

"Do you know what it is?" Sam asked.

"Yes," the man replied, offering no explanation.

"Super," PJ said, "because it's all yours."

The woman met eyes with the creature. "It is ready to fight," she said.

"Yeah, it's got a little anger management problem," PJ agreed.

"Does it have any weapons in there?" asked the man.

"It swings a mean Funny Foam bat," PJ said.

"Yes, they love games," the woman blurted, and the man immediately motioned for her to keep quiet.

"I don't think it was playing a game," PJ said, "unless my head was supposed to be the ball. But don't worry, the bat's not dangerous, just annoying."

"We shall take care of this," the man said.

PJ put the key in the lock. "Good, because I—"

"Arrgh!" The thing in the cell growled and charged up to the bars, snatching the key from PJ. It was out of the cell so fast that PJ hardly had time to turn around before it slammed into Sam with its stout body. Sam flew backward, hitting the wall with a dull thud. He dropped to the floor, stunned.

The creature turned and snatched a fire ax from a hook near the back door with its cuffed hands.

PJ grabbed the first object he could reach to face the snarling beast. He whirled and held up the Funny Foam bat. The ax swung at his head. PJ threw himself to the ground just as it clove the foam bat in half and whistled past his ear.

The strangers threw back their robes.

Shiink! Shhhhink!

The man and woman yanked long, thin rapier swords from hidden scabbards. They moved so fast that Sam only caught a glimpse of their blades as they swung in glittering arcs.

Thunk-thunk!

The creature froze. Black fluid began to spurt from two wounds in its midsection. The dark goo sprayed straight out like syrupy gunk from some sort of grotesque garden fountain, splattering Sam and PJ. Sam tried to scramble to his feet, but he slipped in the rapidly forming puddle and fell belly-first into the sticky muck.

The robed strangers stepped away, their quick and devastating work completed.

The gooey substance continued to spurt from the swaying creature. It smelled like hot mud, and the creature looked like a tree about to fall. The thing's yellow eyes locked on Sam, but they were vacant. It began to shrivel as its vital fluids drained, its skin folding, creasing, and shrinking, and Sam realized that the thing was emptying out. The handcuffs dropped from its thinning wrists to clatter on the floor. Finally, its legs bowed and collapsed, and it fell to the ground, where it curled up like the limp skin of a deflated balloon animal.

PJ and Sam rose carefully, dripping black goo and eyeing the sword-wielding strangers. "I don't think they're from animal control," Sam whispered.

"You killed it," PJ said to the strangers.

"Only because you allowed it to arm itself with an ax," snapped the albino man.

"These upworlders shouldn't have seen any of this," the woman said to him.

"Quiet." The man frowned. "I need to decide what to do with them."

Sam didn't like what he was hearing. They still hadn't lowered their swords.

PJ stood next to Sam and held up the remaining half of the foam bat. "Whoa, there," he said. "You aren't going to get all medieval on us too, are you?"

GOBLINS!

"Of course not," the man snorted. "We don't fight against humans."

"We are servants of mankind," the woman added.

PJ glanced at the limp skin of the creature and the globs of dark blood spattered all over his father's office. "Then are you gonna clean that up?" he asked.

7
BACK TO THE WOODS

Sam rode shotgun as PJ drove his Camaro, and the two pale strangers pouted in the cramped backseat, surrounded by road trip garbage.

"If you are not in charge, you must let me speak to your superior," the albino man demanded. He'd been griping the entire trip and spoke like he thought he was quite important.

PJ slammed to a stop at the end of the road in the woods. "Look"—he turned and glared—"I got a chimp-gone-bad whacking me with a Funny Foam bat. I got you two medieval freaks with togas and swords. And I just spent twenty minutes mopping up the most disgusting goo I've ever seen, felt, or smelled so that my dad, who happens to be the town police officer, won't find it at his place of business. I am not letting you speak with my 'superior' until I figure out what's going on, and probably not then, either!"

Sam watched their reaction. They seemed a bit surprised by PJ's assertiveness.

"Now, the first thing I want to know is," PJ continued, "what in the heck was that ugly, hairy, nasty thing?"

The strangers looked at each other. The man nodded

GOBLINS!

for the woman to remain silent again. She frowned back, clearly wanting to say something.

"Fine!" PJ harrumphed. "I drove you back out here like you wanted. Now, if you and the evidence can just evaporate and leave me in peace, that would be great."

PJ stepped from the Camaro to see if the coast was clear. As soon as he was out of earshot, the young woman turned to the man and pointed out the window. "There is the post in the ground, Whitey. The tunnel is directly beneath it. When we get back down to UnderEarth, we can tell the other soldiers that we caught the—"

"Bree, wait." The man called Whitey shushed her and pointed to Sam, who stared at them over the back of the seat. She'd clearly forgotten he was there.

"Whoa!" Sam blurted. "There are more of you?"

Bree looked at Whitey apologetically. He glared back at her. "That's why you need to keep quiet and let me do the talking," he snapped.

"And you're from underground?" Sam continued. "Man, oh, man! What's it like?"

"Very secret," Whitey growled, showing Sam a dagger in his belt. "Understand?"

Sam shrank away.

"Wait, Whitey," Bree said, and she examined Sam. She gave him an approving once-over and a kindly smile. "This one appears worthy."

"What?" Sam said.

"What?" Whitey said.

Bree winked at Whitey. "I'll wager this fine young boy

has the heart of a warrior. Alas, we cannot take him with us." She turned to Sam, serious. "But we can trust you with our sacred vow of secrecy, can't we, young warrior?"

Sam nodded, fascinated. No one had ever called him "worthy" or a "fine young boy," and certainly never a "warrior."

Bree held out her bare hand. "Okay, then, press your hand against mine and repeat after me."

Sam lifted his hand up carefully and placed it against Bree's.

Clack!

Just then, PJ pulled open the door. "All right, the coast is clear," he said.

Bree gave Sam a quick handshake and nodded at him as PJ ushered them out.

PJ opened the Camaro's trunk and grimaced as they hauled out the limp skin of the creature. It hung like a furry, empty sack in their hands. There didn't seem to be any bones in it. PJ also began to pull out rag after rag soaked with black blood, which he threw into the woods off the path. Bree and Whitey helped at first, but when PJ finished tossing the last soiled rag, he turned to find them holding their weapons. "Hey, easy there," he said, holding up his hands.

"We are preparing to leave, not kill you," Whitey said.

"Great," PJ said. "And not a moment too soon." He lowered his voice. "But, hey, no one can know about all this, eh?"

GOBLINS!

"Agreed," Whitey said. "Tell no one. We will do the same."

Sam had been listening from the car, but his curiosity got the best of him. He stepped around the rear bumper and snuck up on their discussion. Bree and Whitey were standing with their cloaks open, and Sam saw that they wore medieval armor of finely tooled leather underneath—warrior armor. "Cool!" he said.

Bree and Whitey drew steel and whipped their weapons toward the sudden sound Sam made. Their swords stopped just short of his neck.

PJ whirled on Sam too. He stomped his foot, angry. "Watch it! The way these maniacs swing their things around, somebody could really get hurt, like you, for instance, or worse, me! Now, get back in the car."

"But I just wanted to see their swords and the armor—" Sam said.

"No," PJ said firmly.

"And I wanted to know what's in the tunnel under the sensor post."

Bree put her finger to her lips to remind Sam not to talk.

"What?" PJ barked. "Tunnel? No! I don't want to even hear any more crazy stuff. I am not supervising some punk kid on a big adventure to Fantasyland. Ever since I met you, my day's gotten more and more lame."

Sam's grin disappeared.

"In fact, I'm an idiot for listening to a twelve-year-old

loser. Smuggler's loot, my butt! All we found out here is trouble. As soon as we settle this, you're going back to your crappy little cell, then back to your crappy little life."

Sam's lip quivered. It wasn't that he was unaccustomed to being yelled at—his dad did it often. It was just that he thought he'd finally discovered something exciting that he could be a part of. But PJ was right. When the strangers vanished back down the hole in the ground, his life would go straight back to crappy. The thought of returning to his dad's shabby little rented trailer to get in trouble for the stolen fireworks was bad enough. But having nothing more to look forward to than hanging out on the curb at the Stop-n-Sip all summer, and for as far into the future as he could see, was almost more than he could bear.

The warriors were staring at him. No matter what, he didn't want them to see him cry. He blinked back tears, sniffed, and ran off around the car.

PJ turned to Bree and Whitey. "Okay, now you two run off like that and I'll be happy."

"You've seen things you should not have," Whitey said. "You know things you shouldn't know."

"Under the circumstances, perhaps we should ask for his help," Bree said to Whitey hopefully. "He already—"

"Don't be ridiculous," Whitey snapped. "We cannot expect anything from him, except to forget what he's seen."

"Don't worry," PJ said, "you'd be surprised how bad my memory can be when I put my mind to it. As soon as you're out of sight, this is all out of my mind. I don't take on other people's problems."

Whitey nodded at Bree. "You see, he is good for nothing."

Bree seemed disappointed. She looked at PJ, and for a moment their eyes met. Her green gaze was sad, but somehow steady and determined at the same time.

Whitey turned to go and motioned for her to come with him. She looked away from PJ, gave a little wave, and the two melted into the dark underbrush so quietly it was like they were never there at all.

PJ took a deep breath. He found he was waving goodbye to Bree without realizing it. He stuffed his hands in his pockets and walked away.

"All right," he said to himself as he headed back to the car, "weirdos gone, mutant creature melted, evidence cleaned up. Talk about your freaky day." He shook out his limbs to relax. "But it's all good now."

He opened the Camaro door and glanced inside. "Hey, Sam?"

The car was empty, except for the boy's backpack on the seat. PJ grabbed it and looked around. "Sam . . . ?"

8
THE TRAPDOOR

After Sam rounded the patrol car, he dashed into the dark woods about twenty yards away. When he stopped sniffling, he decided he had three choices. The first was to get into the police car with PJ and go back to jail. His dad would pick him up, probably drunk, and he'd really catch it at home. His second choice was to walk home alone. It would be about five or ten miles, in which case he wouldn't have to go straight back to the jail. But Officer Myrmidon would still have to tell his dad about the fireworks, and he'd catch it later. He looked down. His third and final choice lay right in front of him on the forest floor.

The sensor post jutted from the ground. Sam could see its electrical workings through its domed Plexiglas cap. At the base of the post, there was a patch of green grass approximately three feet square. In the dim light of the rising moon that leaked through the trees, he could see that the earth around the edge of the patch was disturbed. The pattern of loose dirt looked fresh.

Sam leaned down and slid his fingers through the tumbled dirt along one edge. There was a lip, and he gave it a tug. The entire square shifted. He felt along the edge to a corner and lifted harder. The square tilted up. It was heavy,

GOBLINS!

but Sam was able to maneuver his hands underneath and heave. Up it went, rotating on a hinge. It was a trapdoor.

Sam pulled the door all the way open and looked inside. The earth was dug out below so a person could drop into a shallow pit. The pit had a round opening on one side. *A tunnel*, thought Sam. It was just like the woman Bree had said.

The tunnel opening faced north, toward Canada. It was dark in the hole, but Sam wanted to see what was down there. Mysterious strangers, monstrous beasts, swords, and medieval armor were far too interesting not to take a quick look. If the tunnel seemed dangerous, he could scramble right back out. He checked over his shoulder and slid over the edge, dropping a couple of feet to the dirt floor.

Sam stared into the dimness of the tunnel opening. A faint greenish glow lit the passage. The compacted dirt walls of the tunnel were perfectly rounded, as though a giant ball had rolled through the earth, and the light seemed to come from patches of phosphorescent lichen.

Sam took a few careful steps. *Nothing dangerous so far*, he thought, *but definitely interesting*. He grinned and began to walk along the passage, which led down, down, down. . . .

9
PJ'S CHOICE

PJ paced beside the sensor post, holding Sam's backpack. Sam had been gone for ten minutes, and the strangers had been gone for five. He didn't know how he'd explain to his dad that he'd lost his only inmate. The truth certainly wouldn't work.

PJ began to practice the speech he'd give his father. "I fell asleep at your desk, Dad. When I woke up, little Houdini was gone." PJ shook his head and tried again. "The kid tricked me into letting him out of the cell, then he overpowered me, and—" *Nah*, he thought. Even if that were true, he wouldn't tell anybody *that*.

PJ was pretty sure he knew where Sam had gone—he could tell by the way the boy's eyes lit up when he spoke about the strangers—and PJ didn't want to go where he was thinking about going, but it seemed his only choice. "Dang it," he mumbled.

PJ began hunting along the ground near the post. He found the suspicious square patch of grass and located the edges. Hooking his fingers under the top layer of soil, he pulled.

It was heavy, but sure enough, the trapdoor of false earth eased upward. Loose dirt spilled into a hole beneath

GOBLINS!

it. Sam had been right. There was a tunnel. PJ had brought along his dad's foot-long police-issue flashlight, and he shined it into the hole. It didn't look like much, PJ thought, but if the hollowed-out space was large enough for a big creature and a robed couple to climb up from, it would be large enough for one delinquent twelve-year-old to climb down into. He took a deep breath and dropped himself into the hole.

Whump! The trapdoor swung closed above him with disturbing solidity. It was cooler underground than up on top, like a fruit cellar. He still had his father's police coat on, and he pulled it tight around his shoulders. "Okay, no problem," he said to himself. But that wasn't true. He'd blown the only responsibility his dad had given him, and he darn well knew he had to get Sam back right away or there'd be a big problem.

10
UNDEREARTH

Sam had been walking for a while. His eyes still weren't completely accustomed to the dimness, but he could make out shapes once he got used to everything looking a bit green. The tunnel continued on, smooth and round, like a five-foot-wide tube. He wondered if it went all the way across the border into Canada.

PJ would probably be missing him right about now, and he would surely get in some serious trouble with his dad for letting Sam escape. *Serves him right for being such a jerk to me*, Sam thought, grinning. He wondered if he would run into more warriors. He'd explain to them that he'd met Bree and taken her oath, sort of.

Sam had walked for at least fifteen minutes down the sloping passage when he saw the light change ahead of him. Sam slowed his pace, but his heart began to beat faster. Twenty feet down the tunnel there was an opening. Sam crept forward and looked out between a jumbled pile of boulders into a massive cave.

"Wow . . . ," he gasped under his breath.

The cavern was the size of a several football fields set end to end, and the ceiling was near his head. It gave him the feeling he was looking down at the vast underground world from the upper cheap seats of a stadium. Inside the cave, the light from the green lichen was enhanced by swarms of glowing bugs that flitted about so that shadows danced and shifted constantly on the massive rock formations that littered the subterranean landscape below. The air smelled ancient and undiscovered, but not stale.

A steep hill ran down from Sam's position for perhaps one hundred yards before a high stone barrier bisected the slope like an underground Great Wall of China. The square wall extended from one side of the cave to the other so that it guarded the hill completely from whatever lay in the caverns below it. There were dark shapes slinking about along the base of the wall and climbing the scaffolding on its near side.

Sam grinned. He couldn't make them out very well in the dimness from the hill so far above, but he was pretty sure they must be other warriors.

Sam left the cover of the rocks that hid the tunnel and started to pick his way down the hill. It was steeper than it looked. He had to move carefully, sometimes forward, sometimes backward, crawling from foothold to foothold so that he wouldn't tumble. As he descended, he wondered if the warriors would have a suit of armor his size and train him to fight with a sword.

Sam was so focused on where to set his feet on the steep, rocky slope that he didn't look up for most of the journey down. But soon, even in the shifting, shadowy light, he was close enough to see the wall and its occupants. He skidded the last few yards, dislodging several rocks. The dark shapes milling around the base of the wall looked up, no more than a stone's throw away. Sam stopped cold and stared. They stared back . . . with huge, pale yellow eyes.

Sam gasped as they came running to meet him with furry, outstretched arms. He turned and tried to run back up the hill, but the loose stones under his feet slid and gave way. Sam scrambled for traction for a moment, then four thick paws grabbed him, and his world went black.

11
GOBLINS

A big crowd of goblins gathered around the base of the wall as two bug-eyed goblin brothers, Nargle and Bargle, hauled a lumpy sack into their midst and hung it triumphantly on a hook.

Sam squirmed inside the dark sack, disoriented and terrified. The goblins had grabbed him from behind and popped him in the bag so quickly that his struggle was a blur.

Bargle poked at the sack like a curious child as more goblins crowded in behind him, grunting excitedly and jumping up and down to get a look.

Suddenly, Slurp, the huge goblin captain, parted the crowd. The others fell silent. Slurp was a head taller than the next-largest goblin. His broad shoulders bulged beneath his thick fur, and his powerful goblin legs were longer and more bowed than any in the crowd.

"Argh!" Slurp grunted.

"Arrgh!" replied Nargle.

"Arghhh!" agreed Bargle.

Slurp champed his tusks and sniffed the sack, concentrating. "Human . . . male . . . child." Saliva flew as the captain spoke, spattering left and right.

Bargle tittered with excitement, his long tongue lolling out of his gaping mouth. He fingered a crooked dagger. "I found it, I get to carve it. General Eww-yuk lets us skin them alive for fun."

"I am not General Eww-yuk," Slurp growled, shooing Bargle and the other goblins back. "We do not torture here. And we kill only what we are going to eat."

Bargle prodded the sack with his dagger. Sam squirmed.

"It does smell taaaaaaasty," Bargle said.

"But it wears strange clothes," Nargle pointed out. "Very-very strange-strange."

Slurp frowned. "Hmmm. Did you tell about this to the Great Goblin?"

"The Great Goblin is too old to be bothered. I sent word to the general instead," Bargle said.

Slurp whirled, angry. "Eww-yuk again? Argh! Tell me first when you find something new! Me! No one else! Understand?"

Bargle winced. "But he is the general, and you are only a captain," he said.

Captain Slurp slugged the sack in frustration.

"Oww!" Sam yelped.

"You tell me," Slurp roared. "*I* tell Eww-yuk. Do I need to cut out your tongue to remind you?"

Bargle pulled out his foot-long tongue and looked at it. "But how wuh I thell you wifout a thongue?" he mumbled.

Captain Slurp's frown deepened. He grabbed his

sword, and it whistled in an arc just past Bargle's tongue to slice through the rope holding the sack. *Snick!* The sack dropped to the ground.

"Ummmph!" Sam grunted.

"Bah!" barked Slurp. "Take it away!"

12
GOBLIN PROBLEM

The tunnel led down gradually at first, then more steeply. Iridescent lichen provided PJ with dim, greenish light so that he was able to switch off the flashlight. "What is this place?" he wondered aloud.

He ambled along, unsure how far he'd come. The cool, closed space and unfamiliar surroundings were disorienting. He cursed himself for not having thought to count his steps. He didn't have a watch to keep track of time, either. *At least there's no chance of getting lost*, he thought—the round tunnel plowed ahead without any offshoots.

After a long series of bends, PJ heard voices and stopped. Ahead, the tunnel appeared to open up into a cavern, and crouched at the opening, with their backs to him, were the two pale humans. Their attention was entirely focused on the tunnel opening. PJ snuck up behind them and eavesdropped. The albino man was not happy.

"It wouldn't have happened if you hadn't filled his head with notions of being a warrior, Bree," he snapped.

"Yes, Whitey," Bree said, "I am at fault. Simply ask it of me, and I shall give my life to retrieve him." She half drew a dagger and rose to enter the cavern.

He slapped her hand. "No. You'll only get killed, and

46   **GOBLINS!**

quickly. A rash, futile gesture does nobody any good. Where's your head at? I'd hoped you would do better on this mission, but I'm going to have to report to our elders that you're not ready for real action. Maybe when you're older—"

PJ coughed to get their attention. "Ahem."

Shhhick!

Before he could blink, PJ was on his back with Bree on top of him and the tip of her dagger at his throat. When she saw his face, she pulled the knife back, though only an inch. "What are you doing down here?" she growled. "You agreed you would go your way."

"Uhh . . . I'm just looking for my bro Sammy," PJ said. "You seen him?"

Bree grimaced and let him up. PJ brushed himself off and retrieved Sam's backpack, which he'd dropped on the ground. He turned to Whitey.

"Sorry," Whitey said, "but he has been taken."

"I am so sorry," echoed Bree, looking particularly guilty.

"Dang it!" PJ snapped. "I don't have time for this. Taken where?"

"By the goblins," said Bree.

"By the what?" PJ asked.

"No, Bree," Whitey interrupted. "We've already told him too much."

"He deserves to know," she said. "It is his brother."

"He's not actually—" PJ stopped and cocked his head. "Wait, did you call those things goblins?"

"You are in their world now," Bree said, and she pointed out into the cavern.

They were perched in the hidden nook where Sam had stood only minutes earlier, atop the steep slope above the stone wall. A series of scaffolds lined the near side of the wall below, providing ladders to the top. Beyond the wall lay a vast, dimly lit cavern underworld with no end in sight.

PJ stared in awe. "Duuuude . . ."

The wall seemed to be designed to guard against whatever was in the gigantic cavern on the other side. The problem was that a large number of dark, ominous shapes were milling about on *this* side. PJ squinted. The shapes were squat, impossibly bulky, and slunk about like hunched apes. He quickly realized they were the grotesque kin of the beast from the jail cell, and they were in control of the wall.

"The boy must have come down ahead of us," said Whitey.

"No friggin' way!" PJ barked. His voice echoed out into the cavern. *Way-way-wayyyyy* . . .

Whitey slapped the back of PJ's head. "Quiet!" he snarled.

"They will have heard that," Bree said, her eyes darting left and right.

"Hurry!" Whitey whispered. "Through here." He darted from the hidden tunnel opening out onto the steep slope and scurried down toward the wall about twenty yards before ducking behind a boulder.

Bree glanced at PJ. "Come on!" When PJ hesitated, she

grabbed his arm and hurried him through the opening to the edge of a steep, muddy path that wound down the hill toward the wall. It looked too slick to climb, up or down.

"Hey, why are we going *into* the goblin cave?" PJ asked.

Suddenly, Bree pushed him from behind, and he plummeted down the wet, curving path like a roller-coaster car. He rushed toward the wall and the goblins, grasping for handholds to stop himself. It was no use. The path was too slippery, and he was moving too fast.

The mud-slickened slide dumped him onto solid ground far below, but well short of the wall. PJ hit the bottom of the slide and lurched to a stop on his back. He sat up in the mud bewildered, until—

Wham!

Bree landed on top of him. She knocked him head over heels, and they sprawled across the dirt. Before he could catch his breath, she hopped up and yanked him behind a nearby boulder. A patrol of five goblins appeared nearby, working their way up the slope toward the hidden tunnel entrance, apparently looking for the sound PJ had made. The goblins stopped and sniffed the muddy chute halfway up, then changed direction and began climbing down toward the three of them, nose to the ground like bloodhounds.

"Good," Bree said.

"Good?" PJ gasped, watching the goblins trudge toward them.

"We've drawn their attention away from the secret tunnel to the surface," Bree said.

Whitey slid behind the boulder to join them. "We'll have to make a run for the wall now and try to break through," he said.

"What?" PJ cried in disbelief. "We were safe up there in the tunnel. Even if they saw us, at least we could have run up and away instead of straight into a fortress full of blood-thirsty evolutionary rejects!"

"Goblins," Bree corrected him.

"They would have followed our scent and discovered the portal to the upper world," Whitey said.

"That's why we came up to pursue the one that accidentally stumbled upon the tunnel earlier," Bree explained, "the one you captured. You must understand, keeping the goblins from discovering the surface is our life's work."

"But it's not mine!" PJ protested.

"Tell him nothing more," Whitey said. "I want him to know as little as possible if he is caught and tortured."

"Tortured?"

"Come. To the wall," Bree said. "It's our only chance now." She and Whitey darted out from behind the rocks.

PJ shook his head. He had no choice. He slipped from the rocks and followed them straight toward the goblins.

13
GENERAL EWW-YUK

In a dark room carved from solid onyx deep in the goblin city of Argh, a slit-eyed goblin sat watching a ten-inch millipede crawl across the floor. The large bug scurried one direction until the goblin's furry paw slammed down in front of it. It turned and ran the opposite way until the goblin's other hand dropped into its path. Finally, it froze, not knowing which way to flee. The goblin grinned, enjoying the creature's fear.

Suddenly, a goblin guard pounded on the door. "General! I have news."

General Eww-yuk swept the millipede up in his hairy paw and popped it into his mouth like a child trying to wolf down a treat so he would not have to share it. "Arrgh!" he replied, crunching his morsel. "Where from?"

A short, thick goblin messenger burst in. "The human fortress wall we took earlier."

Eww-yuk stepped from the shadows. He was a huge goblin and towered over the messenger.

"Ahhhh, something interesting at the wall, eh? And I've left that simpleton Slurp there to guard it."

"He was not wanting to give his find over to you . . . oh, no," the guard said.

"No?" Eww-yuk replied, eyes narrowing.

"Oh, no. Nuh-nuh-nuh-nuh-no."

"Bring this find to me now, if not sooner," Eww-yuk commanded.

"Should I tell the Great Goblin?"

"No," Eww-yuk said quickly. "I will tell him later, maybe."

"Yes, sir," the messenger said. It paused and sniffed the stagnant air. "Are you eating something?" it asked, beginning to drool.

"No," Eww-yuk lied, pursing his lips tight and glaring at the guard.

The smaller goblin groveled. "Forgive me. I am just curious . . . and a little hungry."

"Just bring the thing!"

The messenger recoiled in fear. "Of course. And what of Captain Slurp?"

Eww-yuk turned away and spoke to himself, a habit he'd fallen into ever since he'd killed his brothers. "I should have gotten rid of that mangy rock brain when I eliminated the pups from my own litter," he mumbled.

"General, what of the captain?" the messenger repeated, cringing.

Eww-yuk spat bug juice on the floor and clenched his hammerlike fist. "Bring Slurp here too!"

14
CAPTAIN SLURP

Bree, Whitey, and PJ slid from rock to rock, drawing closer and closer to the wall. Goblins milled about, lounging like off-duty soldiers. They scratched their rumps, leaned against their spiked clubs, and snarled at one another.

"Now what?" PJ whispered nervously.

"We attack," Whitey said. "Rush them in a tight knot. If we break through, Bree can scale the wall and escape into the lower cavern while you and I hold them off."

"I shall fight alongside you," Bree said.

"No, you *shall* not," Whitey insisted. "As long as I am leader, you *shall* do as you're told. You *shall* run, and we two *shall* fight."

Bree looked as annoyed as PJ looked horrified. "Whoa, whoa, whoaaaa there, Mr. Chivalry," PJ interrupted. "Don't go volunteering me for no kamikaze mission. There's, like, fifty of those things."

Bree quickly scanned the goblin positions. "Fifty-one," she said. "He's right, Whitey, there's too many. We must talk to them, trick them somehow."

"They speak?" PJ said, amazed.

"Yes," Bree said, "poorly."

"All right," Whitey snapped, glaring at Bree for questioning his authority. "They've never seen you, upworlder, and they are awed by new things. You might cause them a moment's indecision. In that moment, there is a slim chance that we could all escape. Go ahead of us, walk into their midst, and bluff."

"Whatta you mean, bluff?" PJ said.

"It means to tell them an untruth," Whitey explained, "one that makes them believe that we have superior force, and—"

PJ rolled his eyes. "Duh, I know what it means."

"Then why does he ask?" Whitey said to Bree.

"Because you want me to go first," PJ said, "but I ain't a warrior, I ain't a trained negotiator, and I ain't flippin' idiot. So I ain't goin' first."

"So you will not try to bluff?" Whitey confirmed.

"No!"

Bree looked up the hill behind them. "Sniffers!" she hissed.

The goblin patrol that had been investigating the noise PJ made was coming closer. Two large-snouted goblins had their noses to the trail . . . *their* trail. The sniffers would spot them in moments.

"Then we attack," Whitey proclaimed, thrusting a dagger the size of a letter opener into PJ's hand.

PJ looked up at their numerous enemies. The goblins were outfitted like medieval soldiers, armed with thick clubs, wide battle-axes, long pikes, crude swords, studded maces, and other nasty stone weapons the like of which he had never seen before. PJ looked down at the little knife in his hand. "Dang it, dang it, dang it," he mumbled.

Moments later, PJ strode straight into the goblin camp and walked right up to the biggest goblin he could find . . . Captain Slurp.

Surprised goblins scrambled for their clubs and spears. Bree and Whitey crowded in behind PJ, swords out, guarding his back. They were instantly surrounded by an overwhelming number of furry, toothy soldiers.

"Hey, ugly!" PJ shouted.

Slurp turned. "Arrgh! I am not Ugly," he said, gesturing toward another goblin. "Ugly is over there. I am Slurp!" Then Slurp saw that they were humans, and he grinned . . . until PJ stuck a huge bottle rocket between his squinty eyes.

PJ held the rocket with one jittery hand. He gripped his lighter and Sam's backpack full of fireworks in the other. The beasts were scary enough when they were just grunting, but hearing one talk suddenly made PJ shake in his shoes. He shifted from foot to foot and stared up at the huge goblin, trying to think of a bluff.

"I know what you're thinking," PJ finally growled. "What's this human's problem? Well, umm, Mister Goblin, sir, my problem is I'm a perfectionist, so I've armed myself with the most powerful bottle rocket in the world, just in case I need to blow all your fur clean off. So don't give me and my buddies here any crap, and we'll just be on our way, got it?"

Bree and Whitey both gasped, horrified, as PJ moved the lighter next to the fuse.

Slurp leaned down to look along the shaft of the bottle rocket. He frowned and turned to his soldiers. "Crap?"

Bargle raised his hand and took a guess. "I think it means 'food.'"

"You think everything means food," snorted Nargle.

A second goblin cut in, shouting his own guess. "No-no! It means 'stinky.'"

The goblin crowd began to grow excited. They jumped up and down, babbling.

"Yeah-yeah!" another said. "Extra-stinky!"

"Food!" said a fat goblin, and many around him nodded.

"Maybe it's 'stinky food'!" came a try from the back row.

"I like food!" barked yet another.

Slurp put up a furry hand to quiet the crowd, then turned back to PJ and put his forehead against the point of the bottle rocket again. "Good answers all. Tell me, human, which does it mean?"

"It means if I light this up, you're toast," PJ said, trying to sound as threatening as possible under the circumstances.

Slurp turned to his soldiers again. "Toast?"

Goblins began shouting guesses again like game show contestants.

"Look, you overgrown baboon," PJ interrupted, "it means my friends and I are going over that wall, and if you try to stop us, I'll exterminate you like a bug."

"Exterminate me?" Slurp said. "With this object?" He nodded his thick head. "Ahhhh, *that* I think I understand."

Slurp's huge paw darted out and wrenched the bottle rocket away from PJ, who stared at his empty hand, astonished at the quickness of the hulking beast.

"Uh-oh," PJ whispered.

"Innnnteresting," Slurp said. "How do I make it 'exterminate' something?" The mighty goblin turned the bottle rocket over, poking and prodding at it.

Seeing his chance, PJ flicked the lighter. A small flame popped to life, and he drew it across the bottle rocket's fuse.

Slurp yanked the lit rocket away and reached for his sword. "Do not threaten me with fire, human," he growled as the red ember on the fuse crept up toward his paw. "I do not scare so easily."

Suddenly, the bottle rocket ignited and a great flash of light ripped through the dimness. A stream of sparks and flame erupted from the rocket's tail, shooting out toward the goblin spectators. PJ rolled away, and the backpack full of fireworks fell from his grasp as he scrambled through a gap in the stunned crowd.

Slurp dropped his sword and grabbed the bucking rocket with two paws as it shot flame. The other goblins all hit the deck, covering their heads.

"Run!" PJ shouted at Bree and Whitey.

The rocket burned Slurp's hands, and finally he let go. It flew, screaming, directly into his head and tangled in his shaggy fur.

Bree and Whitey scurried onto the scaffolding, pulling PJ up behind them. They fled past bewildered goblins, up onto the top of the wall. PJ stepped to the edge and looked over. The wall plunged straight down like the face of a tall dam, and it was a long, long way to the floor of the gigantic lower cavern.

PJ turned, dizzy, just in time to see Whitey leap past him, pulling a thin rope from his robe. He looped it around a battlement and, holding tight, flew over the edge.

Just then, a bright light flashed behind them.

Booooom!

"Grab on!" Bree yelled. She handed him one end of her own rope and secured the line to the battlement. PJ hesitated, even as the first crooked goblin arrow wobbled past his head.

Thwi-wi-wip!

Bree waited no longer. She grabbed PJ, hugged him close, and hurled both of their bodies over the edge.

At the foot of the scaffolding, Slurp stood tall among the cowering goblins, shaking his head to rid himself of the ringing in his ears. Goblins began to rise from their terrified crouches as Slurp slowly regained his senses. He realized they were staring at him and reached up to feel his head. There was a huge bald spot where the exploding rocket had burned away his fur.

"It bit me!" he growled.

His soldiers burst into laughter.

GOBLINS!

Slurp fumed for a moment, then snarled at the cackling crowd, "Wait, where are the humans?"

A guard from the scaffolding pointed over the wall.

"After them!" Slurp roared. As his goblins scrambled to gather their weapons, Slurp looked down and cocked his head, curious. The backpack PJ had dropped lay at his feet.

15
A SNACK

Once when Sam was ten, his friend Brian had zipped him inside a sleeping bag and sat on him until he screamed that he was suffocating. That was the way he felt as he bumped along in Bargle's sack—trapped, helpless, and breathless.

He'd lost any sense of direction long ago. He knew initially that the creatures had hauled him to the bottom of the hill and dangled him from something. He'd also discovered that they called themselves goblins. They'd said so as they rumbled and snorted about what to do with him. Sam was surprised that they spoke English. Their speech was thick and sounded vaguely Canadian, but after listening for a few minutes, Sam grew accustomed to their guttural grunting and was able to decipher enough to understand what they were saying, mostly.

It wouldn't do him any good to scream, he thought. There couldn't be anyone around that he'd want to hear him, so he didn't waste his breath. Instead, Sam forced himself to relax. He'd need all his wits and strength if an opportunity to escape arose.

Bargle scrambled across the open plains of the huge cavern on all fours, with the sack strapped to his back. His furry legs rose and fell in rhythm, up and down, up and down, and the cavern floor rolled at regular intervals like gentle waves—a vast sea of ancient lava that had hardened midflow.

Running across the lava fields gave Bargle an appetite, but then everything gave Bargle an appetite. Saliva oozed from between his sharp teeth and ran down his curved tusks, dripping to the ground as he scurried along. Finally, he could stand it no longer and stopped.

"Bargle is hungry," he snorted, pawing at the sack. "Very hungry."

Sam's voice was muffled, but he yelped as loudly as he could. "Hey!"

"A snack, yes?" Bargle said. "Just a little snack?"

"Let me out," Sam demanded.

"Out? Oh, yes. Yes, yes, yes . . ." Bargle drew his crooked knife. "I think I like the thigh meat best."

"Wait a minute," Sam said, realizing suddenly that Bargle was referring to him. "I'm not a snack!"

"Snacks do not know if they are snacks or not snacks," Bargle grumbled.

"You can't eat me. You're supposed to take me to that general guy."

Bargle puzzled over this. "But I'm soooo hungry."

"Listen, you may not eat me. General's orders, right?"

"But just a little nibble of—"

"No!" Sam was very insistent.

"Arrgh!" Bargle threw the bag over his shoulder none too gently. "You are an unfair snack. We will see about this when we arrive. We will see!" Then he started off again, romping across the plains.

16
FIGHT OR FLIGHT

PJ plummeted down the far side of the wall on the rope like a crazed bungee jumper. When Bree and Whitey approached the earth, they swung to jerky stops at the end of their tethers, released their grips, and hit the ground running. PJ clung to Bree's rope and swung for a moment, terrified and light-headed, then dropped off and tried to run after Bree and Whitey. He lurched forward, dizzy, and tumbled head over heels. Bent arrows from above began to clatter on the rocks around him. His robed acquaintances rushed back and pulled him to his feet, and they all ran for their lives.

PJ panted but grinned as they hurried across the open cave floor. "That worked out . . . ," he wheezed, "better'n I thought . . . it would . . . back there."

Behind them, the goblins lowered rope ladders and began to pour over the wall.

Whitey matched PJ stride for stride without missing a breath. "I just thank the good earth that the explosive detonated. At least they do not have it in their possession to copy."

"Who cares . . . about possession?" PJ breathed heavily.

"I mean . . . I dropped . . . a whole bag . . . of them . . . back there . . . but the one . . . I used . . . did the job."

"What?" Bree cried.

Whitey turned a shade whiter than he already was. "They have explosives?"

"Just fireworks," PJ panted.

"You don't understand," Bree snapped. But PJ wasn't listening. He came to a halt and put his hands on his knees, completely winded.

"Don't stop!" Whitey barked.

PJ looked back. They had a good lead on the mob of goblins inching their way down the wall on the knotted ropes. "Just . . . for . . . a moment," he gasped. He was so out of breath he could barely speak.

Bree and Whitey jogged in place while PJ sucked in air, staring at the ground. He found he was standing on a carpet of translucent white grass.

"I'm warning you," Whitey said.

As PJ watched, the grass around his feet slowly grew longer, easing lazily over his shoes. He pulled his foot up, curious. The grass gripped it, but, with some effort, he pulled his sneaker free. "What the . . . ?"

"Move!" Bree yelled.

PJ yanked his other foot off the ground, ripping up grass that had already seized his shoe. He gasped. The root ball of each thick blade of grass was a horrible, round, fist-sized creature with a mouth full of sharp teeth, like a grinning piranha. The grass blades were their tentacles. PJ began dancing a mad jig to shake them off.

Behind them, a goblin archer reached the white field and knelt to shoot. The white grass flowed over its leg, pinning it to the ground. It yelped, then went down thrashing as the carnivorous roots swarmed to the surface and began to devour it like a frenzied school of sharks.

"Keep moving!" Bree yelled. PJ found a sudden burst of energy, and they ran.

Behind them, Slurp grabbed the arm of his fallen archer to help, but it was too late. The archer was already torn open by the sharp teeth of the grass and half drained of its black fluid. Slurp gave a sad frown, then galloped after the humans. His goblin soldiers stampeded after him. Some ran on all fours, like hounds. Others loped on two legs. They were not fast, but they were sturdy and didn't seem to tire. Soon they were gaining.

"Almost there!" Whitey said.

"Almost where?" PJ gasped.

A row of boulders rose up to mark the edge of the carnivorous grass field. Bree and Whitey scrambled over the stone barrier. As PJ stumbled after them, with two club-waving goblins closing in on him, two human archers rose from behind the rocks and took aim. Arrows *thwip-thwipped* past PJ's ears. The two goblins behind him fell, spurting black goo, and were immediately set upon by the grass and devoured.

PJ almost fainted from relief as the archers drew two more arrows. He struggled over the rocks, wheezing from the sprint, while the bowmen sent more deadly shafts out to greet the oncoming goblins. Some of the beasts stopped in the face of the arrows. It was a mistake. The grass rose and dragged them down too.

"Ha!" PJ shouted.

The humans kept shooting. Slurp charged ahead even as arrows whipped past him, still leading his pack of furry soldiers by fearless example.

"Tracker! To the swamp!" Whitey yelled at one of the archers, and to PJ's chagrin, Whitey and Bree dashed off again.

One of the human archers nodded. He was a leathery old guy in worn armor who moved with an experienced soldier's efficiency, but also with the aches of age and too many battles. He hauled PJ to his feet. "C'mon, son," Tracker said with a calm that hinted at many years of experience in life-and-death struggles, "we are retreating."

PJ gulped breaths of air and stumbled after him.

The other archer stayed behind to slow the goblins. She drew her sword and skewered the first two snarling beasts to come over the rocks. Then Slurp arrived. The woman cocked her weapon and whipped it toward the captain's exposed leg, but he was too quick and strong. He brushed aside her blow, heaved her up over his head, and hurled her behind him to his waiting soldiers. Then he climbed up on top of the rocks, towering above the fray. "Wrap it up to eat later!" he commanded.

A short distance away, PJ stopped in his tracks. A vast underground swamp of mud, murky water, and tangled plants stretched before him as far as he could see.

The old soldier, Tracker, didn't hesitate. He plunged sure-footed into the muck and mire. "Stay on the paths," he instructed PJ.

"What paths?" PJ said.

"Look for the mud that holds its shape, and they are easily seen," Tracker said. PJ looked around, bewildered. "Or just grab my belt and walk where I walk."

PJ reluctantly put his hands on Tracker's belt and tucked up behind him.

"He's slowing us down," Whitey complained as they slogged through the swamp. "He has since our unfortunate meeting."

"Yeah, well, I'm not that psyched that I met you, either," PJ said.

They waddled through the muck, Tracker leading, with PJ mirroring his footsteps. As they slogged along, Tracker pointed ahead. "More trouble."

"No way," PJ said. "I've already had the worst day in history. What else could go wrong?"

"Sweeper," Tracker warned.

Bree and Whitey glanced at each other, eyes wide, as Tracker pointed to a smoking slime trail in the mud.

"What's a sweeper?" PJ asked.

"Just stay on the path," Tracker said, "and pray it doesn't come for you."

At that moment, the goblins came sloshing into the swamp behind them. "This way!" Tracker yelled. He launched himself over a dark sinkhole. PJ leapt after him, his trailing leg sinking knee-deep into the muck.

Whitey frowned. "Go! Save yourselves. I'll buy you more time." He turned to face the goblins as Bree, Tracker, and PJ splashed on through shallow swamp pools. When the first goblin arrived at Whitey's position, he feinted with his sword, then darted aside, and the furry creature trundled past him into the sinkhole, where it vanished. *Blurp!*

More goblins descended on Whitey. His blade flashed left and right. The goblins waved their clubs, but he danced and dodged, nimble even in the sticky mud.

Slurp and the rest of the goblins were still negotiating the maze of sinkholes some distance away. For a moment it seemed that Whitey might drive the lead group of goblins back single-handedly. Then the muck around him began to boil.

Suddenly, a huge creature rose from the bog. It was rubbery, thick, and limbless, like a brown slug the size of a city bus. The flesh of its back dripped muck and grime that was perfect camouflage in the swamp, while its underbelly glistened, wet and slippery with steaming slime. Swaying vertically like a dizzy tree, it suddenly fell forward onto two goblins with a meaty *slap!* The ground sizzled, and it slithered ahead, leaving behind two oily patches that were once living creatures.

Whitey scrambled out of the sweeper's reach. The other goblins panicked and fled. Some splashed and floundered through the bog. Others ran into sinkholes and disappeared. *Blurp-blurp!*

Only Slurp stood fast. "Hold your ground!" he cried

to the fleeing goblin soldiers. "Don't be afraid! Close ranks!"

The creature turned toward Bree, Tracker, and PJ, who had stopped to watch from across a large sinkhole. But the sinkhole was no obstacle for the slimy monstrosity, and they all realized too late that they should have kept going while Whitey had given them the chance. The beast was so big and moved so easily in the mire that it was clear it would catch them before they could run even ten more steps.

Just then, Whitey sank his sword into its fleshy under-belly to draw its attention. "Keep going!" he yelled to them. His weapon cut a long gash in the jiggly creature, but the wound closed itself like sliced Jell-O, and Whitey's sword emerged from the caustic flesh melted to a stump. He tossed it down, then leapt across the sinkhole to follow them. The creature reared, surged forward, and caught him midair. Whitey stuck to its slime-covered underside like a fly on a fly strip, and he hung there suspended for a moment. Then the slug thing landed with a tremendous *splash*.

Everyone stared in horror as the creature slid beneath the roiling waters of the swamp with a sickening sucking sound. Whitey was gone. Tracker pulled Bree and PJ away from the horrible scene, and, at the veteran warrior's in-sistence, they fled across the swamp.

17
"A SNACK YOU ARE!"

Sam sensed that things had changed. After hearing only Bargle's heavy panting for longer than his cramped arms and legs cared to remember, other goblin voices suddenly chattered all around him. They had arrived somewhere.

Bargle swung the sack off his back and began to carry Sam like a bag of groceries. These new developments did not comfort Sam, but at least he was not bouncing up and down and bruising all his appendages at once anymore.

Bargle was standing with Brains, a fussy, skinny little goblin with a watermelon-sized head teetering atop his thin neck. Brains pulled out a clever folding stone scalpel from a hidden pocket in his leather tunic. He flipped out the blade and cut a slice in the bottom of Bargle's sack.

Whump! Sam flopped out onto the ground. He looked up, wide-eyed, at the two goblins. Bargle was wringing his hands and licking his tusks with his long, crooked tongue.

Sam jumped to his feet, disoriented, but hoping he could dart in the other direction and escape. He whirled, only to have his path blocked by a goblin far bigger than either of the others.

General Eww-yuk stared down at him. Sam froze and glanced about for any other avenue of escape. Eww-yuk's stone hall was massive, cut from solid rock, and crudely furnished so that it had a cavelike appearance, but a castle-like grandeur. Stalactite and stalagmite pillars jutted at intervals along its perimeter like rows of teeth, so that Sam felt as if he was in the center of a huge mouth. He couldn't imagine how many goblins had spent how many centuries chipping away at the rock to create such a place. The room also had a large door, which, unfortunately, was located on the other side of the goblin general.

Three goblin guards crowded in behind Bargle, staring at Sam with curious yellow eyes.

"Arrrgh! What is it, Brains?" Eww-yuk grinned.

"Human child," Brains said. "Male."

"I can see that much, you brilliant idiot!" Eww-yuk snapped.

Bargle and Brains both cringed. "Sorry, my general," whined Brains, "so sorrrrrry!"

"Have you talked to it?" Eww-yuk asked.

"Yes," Bargle said. "It barks the words 'screw' and 'off' . . . over and over."

Eww-yuk frowned. "What does it mean?"

"I do not know," Bargle said.

"Its clothes are interesting," Brains said, dropping down to the floor to sniff Sam's shoe. Sam promptly lashed out and kicked Brains in the snout. "Argh!" he yelped.

Eww-yuk grabbed Sam by the foot and hauled him up. He dangled Sam upside down, taking his own sniff of the shoes.

"Not made of anything I've ever eaten," Bargle said.

Sam wriggled out of his sneaker and thumped to the floor. Eww-yuk handed the shoe to Brains, who was still rubbing his nose. "Take this and see if there is a use for it." Then Eww-yuk pointed at Sam. "Send that to the meat room. Perhaps it will cook up nicely."

Bargle began to dance in place. "A snack! You see, you see? Bargle told you. A snack you are!"

The idea of being cooked was horrifying enough, and Sam liked it even less with Bargle gloating. Eww-yuk was distracted, still looking at the shoe, so Sam turned to Bargle. "Hey, look over there," he said, pointing across the room at nothing.

Bargle turned to look, and Sam broke free. Eww-yuk had no time to draw a weapon before Sam charged forward and swung a vicious kick at the goblin general, right between his bowed legs.

Thud!

Eww-Yuk grunted, then grinned, unfazed. Sam winced, realizing that goblin anatomy must be a bit different from human, then the three big goblin guards pounced on him.

"This little human seems eager to fight," Eww-yuk said as Sam struggled beneath his goblin guards. "Perhaps we should send it to the arena instead."

18
PJ AND THE GUARDIANS

After PJ and the guardians had waded through thigh-high mud for about a mile, the swamp grew less mucky, less weedy, and less deep. Bree and Tracker moved swiftly onto more stable ground.

PJ stumbled after them, relieved to be out of the mire but haunted by the image of the monster that had swallowed up Whitey. "Oh, dude, dude, dude . . . that was soooo messed up! What was that thing?"

"*That* was a sweeper," Tracker explained with a grim look. "It's nature's janitor. Cleans everything in its path."

"And who are you people, anyway?" PJ said.

"Guardians of the—" Tracker began.

"No!" Bree interrupted. "Whitey ordered me not to tell him anything."

"Tell me what?" PJ said.

"Then why did you bring him here?" Tracker asked Bree.

"I didn't bring him. He just showed up."

"Hellooooo," PJ said, "tell me what?"

Bree ignored PJ and kept talking to Tracker. "A goblin soldier found its way topside. It was dealt with, but it's only a matter of time before the others that came over the wall find the tunnel to the surface."

"And our visitor?" Tracker asked, jerking his thumb toward PJ.

"His little brother wandered down here," Bree said. "He came down after him."

They kept walking and ignoring PJ, so he reached out and grabbed their shoulders to stop them. They half drew their swords instinctively.

"Easy," PJ said. "I'm just tired of you people talking about me like I'm not here."

"I only wish you weren't," Bree said. "You've risked global war."

"Hey, I've lost a kid, and I've lost some fireworks. Besides those two things, I can't see how any of this is my problem."

"Fireworks?" Tracker raised an eyebrow.

"Yes," Bree said. "Thanks to him, now the goblins have explosives and gunpowder."

"Oh, no," Tracker said quietly.

"Oh, no is right," PJ said. "They're illegal and I swiped them from my dad's garbage can. Even if I get out of this mess alive, he's gonna kill me."

"He'll have to wait in line behind the goblins!" Bree snapped. She turned away and walked on.

Bree had remained remarkably cool through all the action, but she was upset now. It was the first time PJ had seen her lose it.

GOBLINS!

"Come," said Tracker. "We need to keep moving."

They arrived at a small, drippy tunnel. Bree ducked inside, and Tracker motioned PJ in after her. The light faded a few feet from the entrance, and the rock floor grew slick and damp, but the guardians forged on, confident and sure-footed. PJ had no choice but to follow their lead. No matter how creepy the darkness ahead looked, nothing, it seemed, could be worse than what he'd already been through.

Bree and PJ followed Tracker into a cavern with a towering ceiling and a maze of spectacular stone columns. He stared up at the huge, dangling cones that seemed to hang from the darkness itself. "Hey, stalagmites."

"Stalac-*tites*," Bree said, shaking her head. She knelt, unstrapped her bow, and drew an arrow, waiting to see if they were being followed by any persistent goblins, while PJ and Tracker continued on.

"These are their brethren 'mites.'" Tracker reached out and patted one of the cones sticking up from the floor. "Like people, no two are alike."

PJ ran his hand over a long, fibrous stone tendril that reached down from the nothingness above to dip into a pool of water. It was different from the limestone stalactites, like a branch, only much longer and hard like stone.

"Woodrock," Tracker explained. "Not really wood, not really rock. It is porous and soaks up the water to feed the living ceiling far above us. We use its water-siphoning arms to make our arrows, straight and true. The goblins use the deep, gnarled roots of burrowing trees that hang in their forsaken caves."

PJ nodded. "Yeah, their arrows suck."

Tracker chuckled, his laughter free and easy despite their perilous circumstances. "What do they call you, upworlder?"

"PJ."

"Ah." Tracker nodded. "Short for pajamas."

"No. It's, uh, short for Percival John . . . but *not* Percy."

Tracker grinned. "I am Tracker, a name given to me by my little brother, Hunter."

"Tracker?" PJ said.

"Short for 'one who tracks.'" Tracker winked.

"What's with the gal who doesn't like me?" PJ asked.

"Bree? She is one of our bravest warriors. She will likely be our leader now that Whitey is gone. She just doesn't realize it yet."

"Her? Your leader? You're kidding, right? She's my age."

"People your age make important decisions. You've probably made some yourself recently, yes?"

PJ looked away and didn't answer.

Tracker continued. "I'm going to tell you something about us, PJ, because I judge that what you think of us is worse than what we really are. Besides, you aren't likely to make it back to the surface to tell anyone."

PJ frowned, but nodded.

"We are guardians of the surface world," Tracker began. "Many generations ago, humans came underground. It should have been no more than a quick exploration, for UnderEarth seemed at first no place for humans to live. But that ancient party of explorers found something."

"Goblins?" PJ guessed.

"Beauty," Tracker corrected him, pointing to the majestic rock formations they passed. "Beyond the dirt were marvelous caverns, great rivers, fantastic creatures, an entire world full of life and wonders."

"And goblins," PJ persisted.

"And goblins," Tracker conceded. "The explorers came across a group of them and drew their weapons. The goblins responded with bare claws and fangs. The humans were equipped with the modern armaments of the times—spears, knives, and clubs. Several goblins were slain and the rest easily driven off. We humans thought ourselves quite superior and safe . . . at first.

"More humans came below. An entire village descended to see the wonders of UnderEarth and lay claim to it. But the goblins returned. Only this time, the beasts were equipped with spears, knives, and clubs themselves. They had imitated our tools, advancing their own weapons technology by centuries almost instantly, simply by observing the weapons the humans had used against them. They also came in a huge pack, hundreds of the slavering beasts. The humans were overmatched. The defeat was quick and decisive. Only a handful of people survived."

Tracker sighed. "Since then, we have existed, the descendants and recruits of those survivors—our ancestors. They hid the tunnel entrance on the surface and became a secret society, one that prevented the warlike goblins from discovering the upper world. We also keep the upper world from discovering the goblins. We have set up barriers at the exits of UnderEarth all over the world, and to this day we guard them with our lives. The hole you found is such an exit."

Tracker looked up. The cavern opened into a brighter cave ahead. "Ah, we are here."

"Where is here?" PJ asked. "And what do you mean by society? And what's with the antique weapons?"

Tracker waved him silent. The cave was alive with swarms of glow bugs. There were voices too, human voices. They echoed quietly but clearly in the tunnel.

Bree caught up to PJ and Tracker. "There is our force!" she said, almost smiling for the first time since PJ had met her.

"At last," PJ said, "some good news."

"Now our veteran fighters can lead us back to retake the wall," Bree said.

Tracker frowned. "It's not that simple."

"But we must," she insisted.

"I don't think you understand," Tracker said, trying to slow her down as she hurried toward the voices.

They stepped into the cave and found themselves at the edge of a modest camp. Blankets were thrown haphazardly on the rock floor and weapons leaned up against the rock walls. A small fire burned in the center of the cave. Bree stopped dead in her tracks and gasped. Fewer than twenty battered soldiers sprawled about, many of them injured, and none of them over eighteen years old.

PJ frowned. "That's it? That's your force?"

Bree stammered. "But . . . but where are all the grown-ups? Where is Yolo? Where is Amadar? Katrine?"

Tracker stepped in front of her. "Bree, after you and Whitey left to chase the first goblin to the surface, more of them poured over the wall. For some reason our lookout didn't sound the alarm, and they overwhelmed us before we had a chance to flee into the escape tunnel. The adults turned and made a last stand among the boulders so that I could lead these young apprentice soldiers to safety here. We made it, but the rest . . ." Tracker shook his head sadly.

Bree pushed past him, in tears now. "Gwen? Lucio!"

PJ shifted, uncomfortable. "Hey," he called after Bree, "I'm sorry. I didn't mean to—"

Tracker put a hand on PJ's shoulder and nodded for him to let her be.

19
DINNER WITH EWW-YUK

Eww-yuk walked to a stone table carved into the wall of the massive dining hall. Other goblins watched him stride across the stone floor, but only Eww-yuk sat at the table. Brains lingered at his shoulder like a little imp.

Suddenly, Slurp burst through the huge doors of the hall. In contrast to the more timid goblins in attendance, he strode directly to the table and slammed his fist down in front of Eww-yuk. "Aaarrrrrgh!"

"Argh?" Eww-yuk replied, looking up, unimpressed.

"You took me from my post!" Slurp barked. "We were just attacked by more humans. They appeared from no-where, like bugs. I lost many good goblins. I must get back to my soldiers who are not so dead."

"Bah." Eww-yuk shrugged. "We have more soldiers. I brought you here so I could thank you myself for turning over the strange human child so agreeably. I'll enjoy seeing him in the arena."

Slurp stared, suspicious of Eww-yuk's tone. "Yes, well, good riddance. Smelled funny, that one."

The head goblin chef, Snivell, came trundling in with a stone box the size of an apple crate. Snivell was rail thin, with paws twice the size of a normal goblin's. Skittering sounds came from inside the box.

"Ahh, will you join us for dinner before we go, Slurp?" Eww-yuk offered.

Slurp, Brains, and Eww-yuk crowded around the table, leaving the uninvited guards to look on with long, hungry faces as Snivell opened the lid of the box and poured its contents onto the table. Creepy-crawly bugs of various shapes and sizes spilled out and began to run in all directions. Some scuttled about on spindly legs like spiders and beetles. Others writhed and slithered like grotesque larvae.

The three goblins began to squash and snatch the little creatures and toss them into their gaping maws. Their lower jaws unhinged like snakes' so that they could stuff the larger bugs down their gullets whole.

Eww-yuk tossed back a six-inch-long beetle, licking his chops. The large bug *thumped* into his hollow stomach. The general patted his belly. "Ahhh, still squirming."

Garfle, snarf, chomp, crunch! They fed in a horrible frenzy until there was but one morsel left—a plump glow bug. The three all spotted it at once. They drooled and eyed one another. A guard who had snuck near the table reached for it.

Eww-yuk's sword whistled from its sheath. *Wiiiiishttt . . . thunk!*

The guard's hand fell onto the table, and he yelped in pain, clutching his empty wrist. Eww-yuk scooped up the glow bug and dropped it into his mouth, munching slowly, savoring it as the maimed guard stumbled to the exit, its arm already deflating.

"Ahhh. Delicious," Eww-yuk sighed.

Slurp grunted with disapproval. "How is the morale of your guards, General?"

Eww-yuk looked up, still drooling. "Eh? What do you mean?"

Brains whispered an explanation in Eww-yuk's ear. Eww-yuk frowned, nodded, and finally understood.

"They know who eats first, Captain," he sneered. "You are free to go now."

As Slurp walked away, Brains stared at the Captain's head. Brains hurried to Eww-yuk's ear and whispered to him again. Eww-yuk's eyes narrowed.

"Oh, and Captain," Eww-yuk called after Slurp.

Slurp turned.

Eww-yuk pointed. "What happened to your head?"

Slurp looked confused. He spun in a circle, trying in vain to look at his own head. Finally, he reached up and put a hand on the bald spot where his fur had been burned away by the bottle rocket. "Oh . . . this?"

"Yes . . . that," Eww-yuk said.

Slurp thought for a moment, a bit of a struggle for him. "Ummm, hmmm." He glanced about nervously. "The battle with the humans!" he exclaimed finally, pleased with himself for inventing an answer. "Yes! Boiling oil. Splat! Right on my head." He forced a laugh. "I almost forgot in all of the war and fighting. Funny, eh?"

"Yes," Eww-yuk said, not laughing, "very funny indeed.

Stay close. We will talk again before I return you to your post."

Slurp grunted and marched out.

Eww-yuk slapped Brains on the back, knocking the smaller goblin to the ground in his enthusiasm. "Good thinking, Brains!"

Brains rose and dusted himself off, while Eww-yuk kept jabbering. "A few moments with him, goblin to goblin, and I can feel that he hides something. I just need you to figure out what it is." Eww-yuk grinned. A large worm that survived the feeding frenzy peeked out between his tusks.

Brains pointed. "General, before we go to the arena . . . you've, uh, got something in your teeth."

20
THE ARENA

Sam found himself in an octagonal room. He'd seen the heavy bar on the outside of the door as the guards dragged him in, so he knew he wasn't going anywhere. His heart had been pounding ever since they'd hit the goblin with the car, and he was tired. He lay down on a stone bench to rest.

For the first time, he wondered exactly how he'd gotten himself into such a mess. *A bunch of bad decisions*, he decided, *one after the other*. He shook his head. *I deserve to be in trouble*.

And he was not just in a little trouble. He was alone in a goblin cell, deep underground, waiting to be thrown in some sort of arena, which was apparently a fate worse than being eaten. But there was nothing he could do at the moment, so he stretched out to try to relax.

Just then the door opened, and a hunchbacked old goblin shuffled into the carved rock room. "Argh," the goblin greeted him.

"Argh," Sam said, trying on their one-word language for size.

The goblin looked at him, puzzled, then laughed. "Arr-ar-arrrrgh." It limped over to Sam and pulled a long, battered dagger out from under its leather jerkin.

Sam's heart leapt into his throat. It seemed the aging creature had been sent to get rid of him once and for all. *I guess the goblins weren't too impressed by my karate kick*, he thought.

But the goblin didn't attack. Instead, it held the weapon out to Sam, hilt-first. Sam hesitated. *Is this a trick?* he wondered. He took the dagger carefully and studied his bent visitor.

"Yesssss," said the goblin, "you could strike. I am unarmed."

Sam debated, feeling the weight of the dagger. It was the size of a sword to a boy of twelve and felt perfectly suited to his small hand. It was as though it had been picked just for him. Sam looked across the room at the closed door.

"Good," said the goblin, pointing to Sam's head. "You think. Is the door locked? Are there guards? Am I ally or foe? You don't know yet, and so you think before you act. Gooooood."

The goblin motioned for Sam to give him the weapon back. Sam shrugged and handed over the dagger. The goblin frowned and promptly whacked Sam on the head with the flat of the blade, then gave the dagger back to Sam. "Never give up your weapon. Never!"

"Who are you," asked Sam, rubbing his head, "and what do you want?"

"Questions, questions. Who are *you*? And what do *you* want, eh?" the goblin replied.

"I'm Sam. And I want to kick your furry butt for hitting me."

"Ahhhh," the goblin said, its yellow eyes lighting up, "a

kick is good, but not in your opponent's furry butt. Do it here—" Faster than the strike of a darting mongoose, the old goblin lunged forward and kicked Sam in the back of the leg, dropping him to his knees. "And here." The goblin planted a foot in the middle of Sam's back and Sam fell to his belly.

The goblin jumped on his back, pinning him to the stone floor. It leaned down, its leathery lips inches from Sam's ear. "I am Slouch," it whispered. "I will train you for the arena. If you listen, you might live."

Sam held the beaten mini sword in his hand. It was carved from the same light, hard stone as the goblin clubs, but it was filed to a point and sharp along its edges. Slouch handed Sam a large piece of tattered leather. It was red-stained, with gaping holes in it. "What's that?" Sam asked.

"Armor," Slouch said, "to protect you."

Sam frowned as the goblin helped him put on the beaten leather jerkin. Finally, Slouch passed him an over-sized rock helmet, which fell down over Sam's eyes.

"When you are in the arena, keep your sword up, argh?"

"Argh," Sam agreed.

Slouch stepped back and studied Sam in his battle garb like a father admiring his son in his first Little League uniform. Sam didn't feel like a warrior. He felt ridiculous. But Slouch nodded, pleased. He turned Sam toward a stone gate.

"And get some fire in you," Slouch said, swatting Sam on the rump. "Audiences like fire."

The gate rattled up. Sam hesitated, but Slouch gave him a good hard shove through the opening, and he stumbled out.

Sam pushed up his helmet, which had fallen over his eyes again, and looked around. He stood in an arena the size of a tennis court. An oval of stone grandstands loomed around it, the seats filled with snarling goblins. Eww-yuk sat in a raised seat three rows up, looming over the event with a huge smile of anticipation on his face. Slurp, the goblin captain, sat slumped and brooding two seats over. Between them was an empty throne.

The audience saw Sam, and a thunderous cheer went up. "Arrgh! Arrrrgh! Arrrrrrrgh!"

Sam didn't know what to do, so he waved. "Argh yourselves," he said.

The goblin cheers redoubled in fury.

"Huh," Sam said to himself, "friendly crowd."

Suddenly, a huge gate on the opposite side of the arena began to rattle upward.

"Uh-oh," Sam said, pushing his creeping helmet back up again.

The crowd went quiet. Sam clutched his sword whiteknuckled. The gate was much bigger than the one through which Sam had entered. Up, up, up it went, and out of the shadows stepped . . . a bug.

The bug looked like a beetle and was the size of a mouse. Sam looked past the insect into the shadows for his real opponent, but nothing was there. The small bug reared up on its hind legs to its full height of five or six inches, indignant and ready for battle.

Sam walked directly to it, dagger limp in his hand. The bug squared off, its forelegs raised to fight. The crowd held its breath. Sam frowned, then he shrugged, lifted his foot, and squished the insect into oblivion.

Spluuush!

The crowd erupted in rumbly goblin cheers.

"Arrgh! Argghh! Arrrrrrrggggggggh!"

Sam looked around, amazed. He'd done it, and he was a star. He waved again, delighting the crowd, then wandered back to Slouch.

"Good-good!" the old goblin said, hobbling about with excitement. "But keep your weapon up." Slouch motioned with his furry arm. "Up, up, up . . . argh?"

"Argh," Sam mumbled, pushing past Slouch. He headed into the waiting chamber, where he sat down, bewildered, and twirled his dagger, wondering what they had in store for him next.

21
BREE

Bree stood before the twenty battered young soldiers. They wore ragged armor, and their weapons hung at their sides, dragging in the dirt. They were older teens, mostly—between sixteen to eighteen by the look of them—but there were younger kids too. The grown-ups were all gone, all except Tracker. The kids' dazed expressions told the story of their devastating defeat at the wall by the goblins.

PJ stood off to one side with Tracker as Bree told them her story. "One goblin broke through and found its way topside," she was saying. "Whitey and I left to chase it before we realized the battle was so grim."

"How was it captured?" asked one of the older boys.

"The, ummm, upworlder captured it, initially," she admitted.

The small crowd murmured and glanced at PJ in wonder.

"He captured it, yes," Bree clarified, "but then he let it escape, and it was killed in the process."

Tracker turned to PJ. "You slew the goblin?"

"I didn't mean to slew it," PJ said. "I mostly laid on the floor."

"We had to save him," Bree added, sounding irritated.

"Hey, I had things totally under control until you two barged in."

"You know what this means, Bree," Tracker said, brightening.

"Nothing, Tracker," she said. "It means nothing."

"He was guarding the portal and captured the goblin single-handed, yes?"

"Kinda," PJ said. "The car helped some."

"And you held the beast captive until Bree and Whitey came."

"And killed it, yeah," PJ said.

Bree opened her mouth to defend her actions, but Tracker cut in before she could speak. "How can you deny it, Bree? He has a natural talent against the goblins. He bested them at the wall too." The aging warrior stared off as he called up an old memory. "It was decades ago when my brother, Hunter, disappeared. . . ."

The young guardian soldiers winced. They'd heard this story before. But Tracker was oblivious and spoke with a voice as distant as his stare. "Perhaps Hunter ran away to the surface. Perhaps he grew up there and is secretly training guardians to watch the portal from above. This could be one of his star pupils."

Bree looked over at PJ, who was absently scratching his butt with one hand and digging in his ear with the other. She took Tracker's arm and carefully shook him from his stupor.

"Tracker, we all love you for the, uh, dreamer that you

are," she said gently, "but there are no surface guardians. Hunter is gone, and your wild theories are merely echoes of your brother's sad memory." She pointed to PJ. "This overgrown child lets his cowardice guide him, and his successes are dumb luck. He wandered down here by accident."

PJ whispered to Tracker, "Did she just call me a chicken in front of all the other kids?"

"I think you are wrong, Bree," Tracker said. "I believe in this boy. I can smell intrepidity on him."

PJ sniffed his own armpits. "Hey, I don't know if I like what you're saying about how I smell."

"Do you forget already that he has given the goblins explosives?" Bree reminded Tracker.

The young guardians gasped, horrified.

"I have not forgotten," Tracker said.

"Oh, man," PJ groaned. "Why do you have to keep bringing that up?"

Tracker turned to PJ. "Because the only thing goblins love more than food and games is gadgets. They do not invent anything themselves. They borrow all of their ideas from other species. They learned how to tunnel from termites. They learned how to blend with the rocks from pill bugs. Their language had only one word, so they stole ours."

"Why do you think we limit ourselves to these primitive weapons?" Bree interjected.

"Because you're backwards-ass creative-anachronism nuts?" PJ shrugged.

"So it must seem," Tracker chuckled, "but not exactly.

We are aware of mankind's technologies, but we do not bring them down here for the goblins to discover."

"They'll study your little fireworks," Bree said. "They'll make copies of them, only bigger. Then they will have gunpowder, rockets, bombs. And when they rediscover the tunnel to the surface . . . just imagine it, goblins running amok topside with those weapons. It will be—"

"Mass destruction." PJ finished the sentence for her.

Bree turned to the remaining young guardians. "Time is short. Whitey is gone. Amadar, gone. Yolo, gone. Who will lead?" The youngsters just stared at her. "Anyone?"

There was a long silence. Bree turned to Tracker, but he shook his head. "You know they don't trust my judgment," he said.

"Anyone?" Bree asked the crowd again. More silence. Finally, a young girl with ragged pigtails raised her hand. Bree took a deep breath, relieved, and pointed to her. "Go ahead."

"I think you should do it," the girl said.

Bree looked around. Other hands went up, voting for her to win an election in which she had not even chosen to run. Soon it was unanimous.

Bree was stunned. "But I'm not ready," she whispered, recalling Whitey's words. "Maybe if I was older . . ."

"Nobody was ready for this," Tracker said quietly, "and they need you."

Bree looked out at the faces of the disheartened teens. "All right, then," she said to the crowd. "I will try to be leader, for now. Just let me think . . ." Her wide eyes be-

GOBLINS!

trayed her uncertainty, and she stood concentrating for a time without saying a word.

PJ couldn't imagine how she could think at all with everyone staring at her, but finally she nodded and spoke. "Okay, a small party of us should retrieve the fireworks before Brains has a chance to examine them."

PJ cocked his head. "Brains?" he said, puzzled.

"The smartest of the goblins," Tracker explained. "Adviser to General Eww-yuk."

"Eww-what?"

"This means finding a way into Argh," Bree continued.

The group erupted into nervous murmurs.

"I will go myself," Bree said. "My brother will not have died in vain."

"Her brother?" PJ asked Tracker.

"Whitey," Tracker said without emotion.

PJ winced. "Oh, man. I didn't know."

"I will guide that mission," Tracker announced. "I am the only one who knows the way."

Bree pointed to a guardian boy who was staring at PJ, fascinated. "Toady, I'd like you to come with us. We'll need a swift messenger if things don't . . . work out. The rest of you follow Braun."

A huge guardian teen with the body of an offensive lineman and a dull look on his face stood up. Bree motioned impatiently for the hulking boy to sit while she continued speaking. "If we are not back soon, you must sneak over the wall and try to take it back. We have to keep the goblins from finding the passage to the surface. We made a commitment, and despite the great odds against us now, we still have that responsibility."

"No way," PJ said. "I'm not going back there to climb a cliff full of goblins. That's insane, man. I just want to find the kid and get out of here."

"Back over the wall *is* the way out." Bree snorted.

She turned away, apparently fed up with him. PJ wondered what she would have been like as a normal high school girl. *Uptight and responsible, probably*, he thought. *The opposite of me.*

"Your brother and the bombs will likely be at Argh, where we're going," Tracker said to PJ.

PJ nodded. "And while we're gone, Brawny here and the others will try to make the cliffs safe for mankind again?"

"We can only hope," Tracker said.

"Okay, then," PJ declared, "count me in for your road trip to this Argh place instead."

Bree frowned, but Tracker nodded his approval. She turned and motioned to the rest of the group. The young soldiers rose, and each shouldered a pack. Two teen boys tapped into the seemingly solid stone wall with metal hand picks and exposed a trickle of crystal-clear water. The rest of the group filed past in a line, filling individual leather skins while a girl of about thirteen set about brushing out their footprints to hide their numbers. They performed these chores so quickly that it was clear they had done them many times before.

When they had finished, they formed into groups of

three and faded quickly and silently into the catacombs, leaving PJ suddenly alone with Bree, Tracker, and Toady.

"I can't believe you volunteered to go to Argh," Toady said, still staring at him. "Wow."

"We're leaving, Toady," Bree said. She jerked her thumb in the direction opposite from where the others had disappeared. Toady hoisted his pack and started down the tunnel she'd indicated.

"Hey, so what exactly is this Argh place?" PJ called after them. But Bree, Toady, and Tracker were already around the bend. PJ rose with a groan and started after them.

22
BIGGER AND BUGGIER

Sam stepped back into the arena, and the crowd went snarling crazy. He waved, winked, and saluted to his furry fans, enjoying his newfound celebrity. He'd been through several matches now, and squashed insect carcasses littered the ground by the opposite gate. None of the defeated bugs was bigger than a house cat, though each seemed a bit larger than the last.

Sam squared with the opposing gate and twirled his sword. The gate rattled up, and a bulldog-sized bug stumbled out. Its plump body teetered on skinny limbs like a fat ant precariously balanced on bees' legs. Sam turned and gave the crowd an "oh, puh-leez" shrug. The bug just crouched there. Sam strutted to it and nudged it with his sword.

Suddenly, the bug spread a pair of hidden wings and flew at him. It buzzed above Sam's lowered sword, splatted his face with yellow goo, and soared over his head. The crowd cheered . . . for Sam's opponent.

Sam stumbled about, wiping the stinging, foul-smelling muck from his face. He cleared his eyes just in time to see the insect dive and swing its heavy abdomen toward his head.

Thump!

Sam tumbled backward and hit the ground. His sword flew out of his hand. When Sam looked up, the bug was upon him again, its nasty stinger raised. Sam scrambled away, his sword out of reach, while the bug chased after him, green droplets dripping from its stinger. He rolled, dove, and crawled to the arena wall.

A laughing goblin leaned down and swatted Sam on the helmet. *Clunk!* Sam staggered along the wall for support. Another fat goblin fan tried the same thing a few rows over, but when he leaned out over the retaining wall, his goblin buddy slapped his back, tumbling him into the arena. The fat goblin flopped into the dirt directly between the advancing bug and Sam. The bug darted at the goblin and flung its stinger forward, stabbing the goblin in the middle of the back. The poison quickly took hold, and the goblin's skin began to progressively disintegrate from the wound outward until, moments later, its innards had emptied into a pile of goop on the arena floor.

The crowd laughed, even the goblin's buddy. Sam did not laugh. He stared, wide-eyed and horrified. As he watched the goblin's fluids seep into the dirt, he noticed that the entire arena floor was multicolored, as though someone had splashed cans of various paints around at random. It was blood, he realized, the blood of many, many different unknown creatures that had died here.

Sam stumbled over something—his sword. He scooped it up as the bug circled around and flew at him again at breakneck speed. When the bug closed in, Sam feinted with the sword and dodged. As it whizzed past, he kicked it in the middle of the back, just as Slouch had taught him. The bug hurtled past him and splattered against the wall, spraying greasy yellow goo all over the front row of goblins.

The goblin crowd cheered him again. This time, however, Sam did not bask in the glory. He hurried back to his open gate, where Slouch waited.

"That thing tried to kill me!" he panted, ducking out of the arena.

"Keep your sword up," Slouch said calmly as he went about inspecting Sam's equipment.

"I was running for my life," Sam persisted.

"You lost concentration," Slouch mumbled.

"I was scared!" Sam shook his head. "Look, I don't wanna play anymore."

"I keep you alive as long as I can," Slouch said, "but your foes increase in difficulty until you meet one you cannot beat."

Sam stood slack-jawed, processing this disturbing news.

Slouch pointed to a bowl of murky water. "You are dry. Drink while they prepare your next match. And remember, keep your weapon up, up, up. Next time will not be so easy."

23
ROAD TRIP

Tracker watched the ground, choosing tunnels with care. Bree and Toady followed while PJ struggled to keep pace. They'd left the pack of young guardians behind just ten minutes earlier for their journey to Argh, and already he was panting.

Soon, the three guardians came to a sheer wall that rose into the dimness beyond their sight. When PJ caught up, he took one look at the looming cliff and figured they'd have to backtrack. To his surprise, Tracker simply took hold of a tiny rock shelf and hoisted himself up. He inserted the tip of his toe in a nearby crack and moved quickly to the next handhold. In no time, he was twenty feet above PJ. Bree began to scale the wall behind him, and she was quicker still. Even Toady had no trouble finding hand- and footholds on the flat wall.

PJ felt for the handholds they'd used so easily but could barely grasp them with the tips of his fingers. He stared up. "Uhh, no way, dudes," he called after them.

Moments later, a long, thick rope slithered down, uncoiling from above, and *thwapped* him on the head. "Oww!"

"Tie on," sighed Bree.

Soon, PJ clung for his life thirty feet up. Toady scurried down to lend him a hand. "We usually stop using ropes around our fifth birthdays," Toady said.

PJ struggled to pull himself up another few feet. "I could climb pretty well when I was five too," PJ panted, "but I'm out of practice, okay?" He drew even with Toady. "So what's your deal anyway, little dude?"

"I'm Toady, the messenger." Toady helped PJ stabilize on a ledge, staring at the older kid with puppy dog eyes. Toady was a long, slight kid who still needed to grow into his body. "I report back to the group if you all die," he said matter-of-factly.

"Die?"

"Yes. Trying to get into Argh is probably suicide . . . let alone get out."

"Why?" PJ frowned. "What is it?"

"The goblin city, of course," Toady said. "Personally, I'd rather storm the wall to the surface by myself with a sock full of rocks than try to get into Argh."

PJ was speechless. He looked behind him. It was a long way down.

"It's very brave of you to come with us," Toady continued. "Perhaps you *are* the hero from above Tracker thinks you are."

"No," PJ groaned, "more like the idiot my dad thinks I am."

24
NO MERCY

Slouch and two goblin guards shoved Sam, kicking and clawing, back out into the arena. Sam stared at the crowd, no longer cocky. He kept his sword up, but his arm shook as he eyed the huge opposite gate. It rattled slowly up, leaving a large black abyss from which two goblins gradually emerged. They tromped out of the darkness, pulling ropes, struggling to haul something out of the shadows behind them.

"Skreeeeee!" squealed the thing in the darkness.

Sam shrank from the bone-chilling shriek. He ran back to his gate, where Slouch watched from behind the bars. "Let me out!" Sam cried.

"Try the leg kick," Slouch said, demonstrating a delicate little ballet-looking maneuver with his crooked goblin body.

Sam glanced over his shoulder. One of the goblin handlers was yanked from its feet and swung by the rope into the wall with a meaty *whump!* The audience roared with laughter.

"Are you crazy? Open up!" Sam yelled.

"There is no reward for running away," Slouch said. "Eww-yuk pays me to see you kill or die."

Then Sam heard something *tromp-tromp-tromp* into the arena behind him. Out of the corner of his eye, he saw the second goblin handler flee for cover. He turned around slowly, and there it was.

The insect reared up, seven feet tall. Its head and armored torso might have been those of a gigantic praying mantis, but its long abdomen was wormlike and had as many legs as a centipede, each with a ragged claw at the end. A pair of larger, grasping mantis forearms pawed the air, tearing at the ropes around its neck. It was the same green color as the phosphorescent lichen from the caverns, except for its head, which was bright red, and giant pincers jutted from either side of its slathering jaws. "Skreeee!" it cried at an octave that made Sam shove his hands inside his oversized helmet to cover his ears. Sam let the helmet fall forward and cover his eyes too, unable to look. The crowd quieted, awed by the insectile monstrosity, and Sam braced himself for certain doom.

But when certain doom didn't arrive, he peeked out from under his helmet. The beast hadn't moved. Sam stared, puzzled, then moved to his right one careful step. The beast moved left. Sam moved left. The beast moved right. Sam frowned. He scampered several yards and raised his sword. The beast moved around the arena away from him, keeping its distance. "Skreeee!"

It still sounded ferocious, but Sam had a hunch. He waved his sword and yelled back. "Ahhhhh!"

The beast shrank away, bleating weakly. "Skree . . . ?"

Sam nodded and approached it, drawing gasps from

the crowd. The huge insect brute backed against the wall, then curled into a ball, cowering. It tucked its head and bulbous eyes beneath its tail, bracing for its own doom.

Sam leaned down and whispered to it. "You're scared, aren't you?" It peeked out with one bulging eye. Sam flinched, and it covered its eye again. Spasms of fright racked the beast.

The crowd smelled blood and chanted. "In-sec-ti-cide! In-sec-ti-cide!"

Sam raised his sword, but he did not strike. The horrible thing was helpless, and he simply couldn't. Instead, he turned defiantly to the crowd. "I will not!" he said. "I will not kill it!" He plunged his sword into the earth in a gesture of peace.

"Arrrrgh!" Eww-yuk roared. The general rose in the crowd, huge among the other goblins. He pointed directly at Sam, and he did not look happy. "Take it to the meat room," he snarled, "now!"

25
THE LABORATORY

After Sam was hauled away, Brains left the arena and headed for his laboratory. The dim goblin lab was furnished with stone tables, stone bowls, carved scales, and other crude scientific instruments. Powders and liquids were scattered and splattered across the working surface. In one corner sat a pile of gadgets—hooks, forks, ropes, and other basic human tools Brains had copied. The original items had been taken from humans they'd captured, and the copies were made from UnderEarth materials. Stone was carved and chipped to re-create human tools made of metal, and dried bug sinew was woven into ropes. Leather armor was imitated too, made from the skins of dead animals like swamp lizards or soft-shell insects.

The entire place smelled of sulfur and other raw chemicals, and the light was brighter than in the tunnels. An enclosed crystal vat filled with glow bugs illuminated the place.

Brains had been waiting impatiently to examine the human boy's strange shoe. Now he trundled up to a table, arghing to himself as he set about dissecting it, occasionally dipping a claw into a pool of green sludge or blowing a puff of yellow dust and watching it settle on the sneaker. He carved off a piece of leather and tested its strength, then licked it with his long, curled tongue. "Hmmm," he mumbled, "animal skin."

He investigated the shoe's rubber sole. This was a greater mystery. Water beaded up on its surface and ran off, but the powder clung and caught in the design stamped in the flexible material. He poked, prodded, and stared for a long time at the intricate pattern until his bulging eyes swam. Finally, he picked up the shoe and slammed it on the stone countertop. The shoe rebounded and whacked his pudgy nose in the exact spot where Sam had kicked it. "Arrgh!" he yelped, and he danced about holding his snout. In his anger, he grabbed the shoe again and took a chomp out of the sole. He calmed, teeth champing up and down, a curious look on his face.

"Hmmm." He nodded. "Chewy, very chewwwwy."

26
REST STOP

PJ dragged himself up over the crest of the cliff wall with the help of all three guardians. "Are we there yet?" he gasped.

Tracker grinned. "Just ahead."

Another massive cavern opened up over the top of the wall. In its center stood a stone column fifty yards wide that supported the main cavern ceiling. An underground river tumbled from a hole in one wall and ran in a circle around the column like a dark moat before it disappeared into the gloom on the other side.

"Whoa! Now that is way cool," PJ wheezed.

Toady nodded. "Way cool."

"Don't start acting like him," Bree scolded. She edged out onto the open plain, eyes darting about as she scanned the cavern.

"Bit uptight, isn't she?" PJ said quietly to Toady.

"She's a great warrior," Toady replied.

"I don't get it," PJ said. "Why not Tracker for leader?"

Toady looked around carefully to be sure Tracker was not within earshot. "After his father was killed and his brother, Hunter, disappeared with nothing but his armor and sword, everyone felt Tracker became a bit . . . erratic."

Suddenly, Tracker popped out, camouflaged almost completely in his gray cloak beside a boulder immediately behind Toady. "He means crazy," Tracker said, flashing a crazy grin. The crow's-feet around his eyes deepened. He looked about sixty years old, just a few years older than PJ's own father, and he had lots of miles on his worn face. "They all think I'm a wacko. And maybe I am. Don't worry, though—Bree is a capable young woman."

"Yes," Toady said, sheepishly agreeing with the elder guardian, "I would die for her."

Tracker flashed an even wider grin. "And you very well might."

The new cave sloped gradually down. They wove through the rock formations to the bank of the spectacular river, which looked like a huge black snake slithering through the cavern. PJ bent and flicked his hand through the inky current. The water was not black, but instead sparkled like crystal in the dimness as it dripped from PJ's fingers. It looked black in its bed because the dark ground under the water was devoid of glowing lichen.

Bree, Tracker, and Toady hiked ahead and waited at a shallow ford in the river for PJ to catch up again. Bree frowned.

PJ put his hand up to stop Bree before she could complain. "I don't mean to bitch," he panted, "but we've been fleeing, climbing, crawling, and spelunking like we're in a flippin' underground iron-man race. And I haven't trained for it." He stopped to put his hands on his knees and breathe. "Think we could rest again for, like, two seconds?"

Bree sniffed. "Do you think the goblins are resting right now?"

"Probably," PJ said. "It's not like they screwed up and have to recapture *their* fortress."

Bree bit her lip. She unclipped her sword belt, threw it to the ground, and stomped off.

"Good news," Tracker said. "That means we're stopping to rest."

PJ plopped down and sprawled out. Tracker squatted, at ease but ever alert. His thick leather armor was so well worn that it seemed to bend and move with his body. It was as though the things he wore were a part of him, and PJ wondered if he ever took them off.

Toady crept up and examined PJ's clothes, just as curious.

"What's it like up there?" the guardian boy asked.

"Huh?" PJ turned and found Toady pawing the nylon police jacket he'd taken from the cruiser.

"Toady's indigenous," Tracker explained. "Born down here. He's never been topside like some of us have."

"Where are his folks?"

"Eaten years ago by the goblins."

PJ winced. "So you've never seen the sun, Toad?"

"I've heard of it. Does it really burn your eyes out?"

"Only if you look right at it." PJ shrugged. Toady shivered and stopped asking questions.

PJ turned to Tracker. "I don't understand. Why don't we just, like, get some industrial-strength pesticide to take care of this goblin problem?"

Tracker laughed. "Destroying them is not so simple. Argh is but one nation of an entire underground world of goblins. Their caverns run throughout the earth. It would be like trying to kill all of the world's rats. Besides, why go to war with an entire species when we can coexist by simply keeping them contained?"

PJ nodded.

"The balance has been kept for generations," Tracker continued, "a few humans posted at the various exits around the world keeping the goblins from getting up top. We only lost our fortress here because they somehow discovered grappling hooks and learned to climb the sheer, polished wall."

"Why do you keep them secret from the rest of the world?" PJ asked.

"People are too curious. They'd be down here upsetting the balance. Are you old enough to recall the hysteria about Bigfoot?"

"No way," PJ gasped. "A goblin?"

"Got loose on the surface for days," Tracker said. "Had to go topside and do some fast tracking that week. Thankfully, we found it before you upworlders did. We pulled a couple of crude hoaxes to throw you off the track."

"Now you're yanking my chain." PJ grinned.

Tracker pulled his leather armor over his head and demonstrated a shambling walk, swinging his arms—the famous Bigfoot walk that PJ had seen on old videos.

"That was you?" PJ exclaimed.

"You've heard of the Yeti in the Himalayas?" Tracker

said. "Same thing, although our Asian sect dealt with that one. There's even an ancient legend that the Romans discovered a great ape-dog that could talk and, thinking it an abomination, they used it for sport in their coliseum. Sounds an awful lot like our furry friends down here, eh?"

PJ shook his head, fascinated.

"Imagine the many different governments of our world confronted with news of a new species that has a nasty habit of dining on us. What would they do?"

"Slaughter them, make fur coats, eventually put the survivors in a wildlife preserve," PJ said.

"Ah, yes, a wildlife preserve. And is that not what we are doing by keeping them contained down here? Only there is much less of this slaughter business. We fight with the goblins only when necessary, but sometimes we have to kill a few of them. And they have killed some of us over the years." Tracker suddenly looked sad and angry at the same time. He quickly added, "But we primarily have tried to keep them safely behind the wall."

"You make it sound like you're the guardians of the goblins, not us."

"It can sound that way, yes. But in a full-scale war there would be great losses on both sides." Tracker sighed. "And don't be so sure humanity would win. Goblins assimilate very quickly. Each time we have defeated them, they have learned from it and come back stronger in the next battle."

PJ listened with an uncharacteristic serious expression, while Tracker pulled his sword and ran his finger along the edge of his blade, testing its sharpness. There was an inscription near the hilt—his name, Tracker. It seemed a guardian's sword was a very personal thing, something they held close and wielded like a fifth limb. "So, Tracker," PJ said after a time, "how did you become—"

"A guardian?" Tracker said without looking up. "Nobody makes us stay down here. Over the years, some have chosen the surface and a life in the sun. But my father was a guardian, and his father, and his father, all great swordsmen. My father was an expert tracker too, a real hero to me. And didn't you ever want to be like your father when you grew up?"

"My dad?" PJ shifted uncomfortable. "Ha! No way. My mom's an artist, and she had this great career opportunity far away in Los Angeles, but he let us go down there alone just so he could keep his stupid job up here. When Mom got successful, he still didn't come down to join us. Said he had a commitment and responsibility here as the dorky Sheriff of Nothingham."

PJ looked down and kicked a stone across the cavern floor. "Nah, your dad was, like, this loyal warrior fighting for the good of mankind. My dad's just not that cool."

27
TOO MANY COOKS

Sam hung upside down in the meat room alongside dozens of dangling bug carcasses. After he'd spared the huge bug's life, they'd dragged him from the arena, but not very far. They'd thrown him in here, where he'd almost gagged at the sight and smell of the hanging bug bodies, and trussed him up with coarse rope. The walls of the cave were carved out, but rough, not smooth as they had been in the hall where he'd kicked the goblin general in the crotch. Blood rushed to his head, making him dizzy. He felt like he was in a dream. More like a nightmare. *Maybe I'll wake up*, Sam thought hopefully.

Just then, three goblins burst through the door. They carried nasty cooking implements—barbed tongs, a serrated cleaver, and something that looked like a large stone spork. Sam stiffened, hoping that they were there for one of the other hanging slabs of meat.

The goblins began to stalk through the swinging dead insects, poking and prodding. They muttered to one another, debating the virtues of this or that cut of bug flesh. Through their chatter, Sam was able to make out their names. Snivell was a cook. He carried the tongs, while Blug swung the notched cleaver back and forth, and the one called Guh-wat seemed to take pleasure in jabbing his three-pronged spork into the tenderest parts of the dead hanging animals.

Sam watched in horror as Snivell turned his bulbous eyes toward him and grinned.

"Argh!" Snivell said.

"Arrgh!" Blug added.

"Arrrgh!" Guh-wat said, which appeared to bring them to a consensus. They hustled over to Sam.

Snivell giggled madly. "Let's roast it," he said.

Blug shook his thick head. "Naw, let's skewer it."

"Let's skewer *and* roast it," Guh-wat suggested.

Blug and Guh-wat rumbled with laughter.

"I think we should kill it too," Blug said.

"That's the whole point of roasting!" Snivell explained, waving his tongs in Sam's face.

"Except for eating," Guh-wat said with a concerned look. "That's part of it too, eh?"

Guh-wat and Blug hopped up and down, excited by the suggestion of eating. Snivell tapped the exoskeleton of a giant insect hanging beside Sam. "These you cook right in the shell," he said, displaying his expertise in cookery to his two hungry colleagues.

Sam didn't like the way they were holding their utensils. "Hey, uh, can we discuss this first?" he said.

"Quiet! We don't talk to the food," Blug said.

Snivell nodded. "A human once talked his cook into letting it loose. They're wily, they are."

"Eww-yuk found out and had him hunted down with spears," explained Blug. "Very messy."

"Later, they hunted down the human too!" added Guh-wat.

"Cooked it up nice and tender," Blug said.

Snivell flashed Sam a dirty look. "So don't get any ideas!"

Sam eyed Snivell. The skinny goblin had the manner of one who doubted his own authority, and Sam wondered if his uncertainty could be used against him. "Okay," Sam said, "I don't want to talk to *you* anyway." Sam winked at Guh-wat so that Snivell could see him do it.

Snivell nodded at first, satisfied, but then puzzled over the wink for a moment and frowned. "Wait. Why don't you want to talk to me? You got a secret you're not telling old Snivell?"

"Maybe," Sam said.

"Eh?" Blug said, also becoming interested. "Really?"

"Maybe not," Sam taunted.

"Are you gonna tell me?" Guh-wat said, dancing back and forth like a child that has to use the bathroom. "Just me? Is it a human secret? A new one that nobody knows yet?"

They were curious, nosy beasts, and Sam made them wait, letting their minds turn for a bit and wonder what he knew that they didn't. They crowded around him, jostling and elbowing each other out of the way to hear him. Now all he had to do was think up a secret.

"Tell me!" shouted Blug. "Tell me!"

"No, me," Snivell barked. "I am the cook here! Is it the way to prepare you for stew? How to make your meat the most tender?"

"He doesn't want to talk to *you*," Guh-wat snapped, shoving Snivell backward.

Sam just hung there upside down and pushed his hands up into his pants pockets. Suddenly, his fingers closed around something that gave him an idea.

28
SLURP'S SECRET

After the events in the arena, all the goblins emptied into the city's catacombs to sleep, eat, and yammer about the strange human boy who had refused to kill his final insect foe. Slurp made his way to his bedchamber in the tunnels beneath the city. He was weary from the earlier battle with the humans at the wall and the later chase through the swamp.

Slurp's chamber was little more than a dirt cave. A rock shelf protruded from one wall like a crude, uncomfortable jail cot. Slurp approached the shelf, checked over both shoulders, then pulled the bag of fireworks from under the cloak he wore over his armor. He removed a bottle rocket similar to the one that had blown a patch of fur off his head. He handled it carefully and examined it with great curiosity. It could be a grim weapon, that was clear. Slurp was not certain what had made it fly or explode into a ball of flame, though he knew it had something to do with the small fire the human had held in his hand. But the gadgets could not be turned over to Brains, who served Eww-yuk. The power-hungry general would surely find some way to rob Slurp of the find, as he had the human child, and put the dangerous things to ill use.

Slurp thought for a moment that he might take the find to the Great Goblin. But the Great Goblin was old and less interested in gadgets now than was normal for a goblin. Strangely, as the ancient ruler began approaching his time of death, he had taken to puzzling over philosophies about life and never left his great hall. Very ungoblin. It was a sign of a fading mind, Slurp thought.

He snorted. It was well known how unhealthy it was to think outside of the present or to live according to anything but what lay in front of you. To stay sharp, strong, and ready to react, a goblin had always to focus on the simple and not get caught dreaming or pondering. It was like the old goblin saying: "The rocks will outlive we beasts who think too much." The saying had originally been simply "Argggh," but using the human language had made it longer and more complicated.

Slurp put the bottle rocket back in the bag. Its mysterious power was unsettling. He would decide what to do with it later. For now, it was only important that it was a prize, one not to be surrendered to his scheming superior.

Slurp stuffed himself under the shelf in a tight ball, as goblins did when they slept. When he had settled in, his fur blended with the surrounding stone so well that he looked like little more than a dark lump of rock. He placed his singed head on the bag of fireworks and fell into a fitful sleep.

29
A NEW GAME

Snivell, Blug, and Guh-wat sat cross-legged on the floor as Sam dealt each of them a hand of blackjack from the deck of cards he'd been carrying in his pocket ever since he'd been thrown in jail.

"No." Sam shook his head. "It's not like the last game I showed you. In this game, you count up your cards."

"I have two!" Blug grinned.

"No, no. The symbols on your cards," Sam corrected him.

Guh-wat grunted, perplexed and annoyed.

"Guh-wat can't count," Snivell said.

"That's okay, you guys can help him," Sam said.

"But I don't want to help him," Snivell whined. "I want to help myself!"

"No. You're all trying to beat me."

"I like this game," Blug said.

"Yes," agreed Guh-wat, "let's call it, 'Beat the Human.'" They all laughed and pounded their utensils on the floor with animalistic glee.

"Argh!"

"Arrgh!"

"Arrrgh!"

A bell sounded in the distance. *Clang! Clang! Clang!*

"Uh-oh." Snivell frowned. "Time to go."

Guh-wat threw his cards down. "Argh!"

"I was just getting the hang of it," Blug complained. "Look, I have ten and five. I only need a few more!"

"The bell means come," Snivell said. "Make no mistake. Clang, clang, clang—come, come, come. Eww-yuk uses the bell we took from the human wall to signal an attack!"

"C'mon . . . hit me," Blug said. "Just once."

"Eww-yuk would do more than hit you if he learned that we learned something new without learning it to him," Snivell said.

"He'd flay us alive!" Guh-wat cried.

"Argh-argh-arrrrrgh," Blug mumbled.

With that, they all rose reluctantly and headed for the door, seemingly forgetting Sam. Sam rose too, collecting the cards and waiting nervously to see what would happen next.

Suddenly, Snivell turned back and saw Sam standing there unchained. "Wait a minute. . . ." His narrow eyes narrowed more. "Oh, but you're clever, you humans."

"Yes, very clever," Blug agreed.

Snivell pointed a long, skinny finger at Sam. "Thought you could outsmart ol' Snivell, eh?"

"And Blug too?" Blug said.

"A dung frog could outsmart you, Blug," Snivell said,

and he snatched the deck of cards from Sam's hand. "*We will hold on to these!*"

They exited, cackling at their cleverness. The door banged shut, and Sam looked around, dumbfounded that they'd left him unhung, with his arms and legs unbound.

30
DETOUR

After Bree, PJ, Toady, and Tracker washed swamp goo from themselves in the dark water, the group pushed onward. They made good time across the flat cavern beyond the river. Even PJ picked up the pace.

Presently, they paused, and Tracker knelt to feel the ground. Bree, PJ, and Toady waited as he lay down and put his face next to the earth. He stretched out, completely prone, and held himself motionless for a time.

"Why are we stopping again already?" PJ said. "I'm rested now."

"Shhh. Tracker is reading the earth," Bree said.

Tracker spoke from his prone position. "A goblin army has passed here."

PJ glanced around. The dusty cavern floor was covered with black goblin hair and footprints. "Good guess," he said.

"There were many of them," Tracker continued.

Even PJ could see the horde of footprints. "No offense, but these aren't exactly revelations."

Tracker continued to concentrate. He sifted goblin debris through his fingers. Finally, he nodded, satisfied, and rose. "One hundred and twenty of them . . . er, no, twenty-one. Fifteen in heavy armor, ten archers, and five pack slaves. The rest in leathers." Tracker sniffed a clump of hair. "Eww-yuk's soldiers." He tasted it. "They ate recently. Roast beetle . . . a little undercooked."

PJ stared, amazed. Toady shrugged as though the wily old soldier had done nothing out of the ordinary. Bree just smirked at PJ.

PJ shook his head. "Wow, dude. That was amazing."

Tracker pointed to a large opening in the cavern wall some distance ahead. "We must steer clear of the goblin gates inside that cave. With this number of soldiers on the march, they will have sniffers out prowling for the scent of anything within a mile. We must take a different path."

Bree frowned. "You don't mean . . ."

Tracker gave her a solemn nod.

"Mean what?" asked PJ. "Tell me what's going on this time!"

Toady turned to PJ. "Bug tunnel."

"Bug tunnel?" PJ repeated. "That doesn't sound too good."

Tracker began walking and motioned for them to follow. "Come. It's the only other way to Argh."

"What's a bug tunnel?" PJ insisted.

"A tunnel," Bree said.

"With bugs," Toady finished.

"Like creepy, slimy, disgusting ones?" PJ said, cringing.

"Just keep moving," Bree said.

"I'm not sure I prefer this bug thing over goblins," PJ said. "I have a real problem with insects."

"The gates are well guarded," Bree said. "We'd be captured. Do you know what goblins do to humans they catch?"

PJ gave her a blank look. "I guess the answer'd be . . . nuh-uh."

"They eat you. But sometimes they cook you first. And for that, they prepare you by skinning you, tenderizing you, and chopping you into bite-size pieces."

PJ winced. "Okay, okay. Bug tunnel it is."

31
LIVE MEAT

After the cooks left, Sam roamed free in the meat room. Chilled air swirled about him, and he shivered. The cavern had a natural breeze that kept it a few degrees cooler than all the other caves he'd been dragged through that day. Sam soon realized that the room had been chosen for storing dead animals because the cool temperature would keep the meat from spoiling quickly. From the occasional waft of putrid smell, however, Sam thought it was probably not doing its job one hundred percent.

Sam tried the door. It didn't budge. There was only one other option. He'd have to explore the grim room. He began to creep around the perimeter of the irregularly shaped cavern seeking another exit, navigating the forest of hanging carcasses and gingerly pushing them aside when they hung too close together for him to pass. He crossed one half of the room and found nothing, then took a deep breath and squeezed through two gigantic beetles to try the other side. He shouldered a dog-sized moth out of his way, and a bigger body swung into his path. The large thing spun on its rope so that it turned to face him.

Sam gasped. It was a dead human.

The lifeless person was a freakish-looking guy with a

ponytail. He wore spelunker clothing and looked fresh, if there was such a thing as fresh among corpses.

Aghast, Sam turned and ran, bumping through hanging slabs of insect meat until he slammed into the far wall. He breathed hard and clawed his way along the wall, wanting to get as far away from the human body as possible. His only choice was to squeeze through death, stench, and exoskeletons until he found himself in the farthest corner of the rough-cut room.

When he turned to face the wall, he found himself staring at another door. He tried it. It opened, and he burst out of the meat room, thinking that whatever was waiting in the next cavern couldn't be any worse.

Sam found himself standing in a large, open cave. Again, it was rough-cut, not carved like the more formal halls. A series of stone half walls around the edges of the room divided the space into what looked like animal pens, each bigger than the last.

A long pole with a loop of rope at its end hung on the wall beside the door he'd come through. Sam took it down and held it in front of him for protection. He wasn't sure what it was, but he was beginning to have a bad feeling about the room.

He couldn't quite see over the walls and into the pens from where he stood, but he heard a skittering sound, then a high-pitching tittering. *Yep*, he thought, *a very bad feeling.*

Suddenly, noises seemed to come from everywhere. It was as though his presence had awakened the room. The air buzzed with low hums, shuffling, chirping, and other sounds Sam could not even name. Eyes began to appear in the dimness, lots of eyes, staring at him from over the walls of the pens. He reached behind himself to check the door he'd come through. If nothing else, he could retreat to the meat room, where at least everything was dead.

His hand gripped something that felt like the round rod already in his other hand, but he didn't recall seeing two. He risked a peek over his shoulder and gasped. The "rod" was a long, spindly leg. He let go and stumbled backward into the aisle between the pens.

Perched over the door just above his head was a monstrosity so hideous that he almost screamed. It was obese and bloated—the size of an overstuffed chair—and it hung upside down from the ceiling by multiple spiderlike legs. But it was not a spider. Its horrible mouth was round and lined with nasty, needle-sharp teeth, like those of a leech.

Startled, the creature over the door scurried up to the ceiling with a speed that belied its great bulk. It retreated to a dripping, sticky nest three times its own size that stretched from the top of the door to the ceiling above it. Protruding from the nest were legs and antenna from other insectile creatures—its victims' body parts. Sam saw a deflated goblin arm also woven into the fabric of its grotesque home. Its diet was not only other bugs.

The creature hung, watching him with large, dispassionate black eyes. Sam risked a look around. He could see over the low walls now. The pens on either side of him were filled with bugs. Long, yellow, maggot-looking worms squirmed in one, while another contained hopping beetles. The beetles leapt about with excitement, smacking into the walls of their pen and each other, their legs not quite powerful enough to propel them clear of the pen wall. *A smorgasbord for the thing over the door*, thought Sam, *which is probably why it's so fat*. He looked up, but in the instant he'd looked away into the pens, the thing had disappeared.

Sam glanced about, petrified. The ceiling was honeycombed with sticky, dripping debris. The thing might be anywhere and well hidden. He held out the pole with the loop of rope like a weapon, backing slowly away from the door.

Movement above him in the shadows caught Sam's eye. The thing was tracking him, flitting between the dark recesses in the rough ceiling, hiding its bulk in the empty black spaces. Sam could guess its path now as it appeared and disappeared. It was herding him toward the far end of the cave between the crowded pens. In that narrow space, he would have no room to duck or dodge out of the way when it dropped on him like a plump, hungry recliner.

32
BUG TUNNEL

Bree, Toady, and Tracker arrived at a dark tunnel and peered inside. It was round and five feet wide across the middle, but much narrower at the bottom. The glowing lichen that covered the walls of the larger caverns was nowhere to be seen inside. The rock surfaces near the entrance of the tunnel were smooth, as though picked clean.

"Bug tunnel, eh?" PJ said, popping up over Tracker's shoulder to take a look. His voice bounced into the blackness and rattled around like a marble dropped into a metal pipe. "It's dark in there."

"Bugs eat the lichen," Toady said, "some of them."

"Looks like any other creepy tunnel I've seen down here, only darker."

Bree shushed him. She grabbed the flashlight from his belt and shined it on the wall. The smooth rock face was interrupted every few feet by holes as perfectly round as the tunnel itself.

"Bug burrows," Tracker said.

PJ pointed to a huge three-foot hole. "That size?"

Tracker nodded. "I know they look small, but it's amazing how bugs can squeeze down into them."

PJ gulped. Bree swung the flashlight along the rows of small and large holes that honeycombed the tunnel. Antennae protruded from some of the dark spaces. One pair looked like bare, motionless sticks, while another looked like feathery branches the size of tennis rackets. They waved without wind, testing the air for enemies, or prey.

"Tell me we're not going through there," PJ said.

"I'll go first," offered Bree.

"No," Tracker said. "I've been through here before, and back. The rest of you follow me, and step exactly where I step."

He slid into the tunnel, and Toady eased in after him. Bree nudged PJ. "You're next."

"Why am I next?" PJ asked.

"Because I'm going to watch the rear," Bree said.

PJ stepped into the tunnel, but hesitated. Bree poked him in the butt with her dagger. He winced and hopped forward.

The four of them crept down the tunnel, all placing their feet in the same spots. They squeezed past searching antennae, ducked under strange, sticky webs, and steered clear of the larger holes.

Then Tracker stopped. He pointed at two very big holes, one on either side of the tunnel. Huge antennae protruded from each, waving across the tunnel like sweeping trip wires. "Grabbers," Tracker whispered. He stood motionless, evaluating their choices, watching the antennae drift back and forth.

There was not much room to squeeze past them, but

there was a rhythm to their motion, and every fifth pass or so there was an opening between them. Tracker watched, trying to get a feel for the timing. He watched, and watched . . . and watched.

PJ fidgeted as he waited. He saw a small hole to his left and shined his flashlight into it. A poodle-sized bug gazed out at him. It was motionless, so PJ leaned closer to see if it was dead. Suddenly, it gnashed its pincers and darted toward him.

PJ jerked away, but the bug had only feinted at him and never left its hole. PJ, however, stepped backward, nudging Toady into one of the huge, waving antennae.

The grabber bug struck like lightning, shooting from its hole and clasping two powerful forelegs around Toady's chest. Toady had time only to reach out for PJ before the bug pulled him away, yanking him headfirst into its hole.

"No!" barked Tracker, and he dove into the hole after Toady, his small dagger drawn. PJ whirled, stumbling right into the other set of antennae.

The second grabber bug struck from the other direction. But Bree's sword was quicker. *Thunk!* The head of the attacking bug fell to the ground just as PJ felt its clasping legs brush against his shirt.

Drawn to the commotion, other bugs began to emerge from their holes. They crawled toward the group while Bree and PJ turned their attention back to Toady's bug hole. They heard the sounds of struggle inside. *Thunk- skitter . . . thunk!* Bree shoved her arm into the hole and fished around in the blackness. PJ was almost certain she was going to lose her hand.

Suddenly, she yanked, and Tracker tumbled out with Toady in a lifeguard carry. Both were covered in green bug guts.

"I'm sorry," PJ spluttered. "I'll stay in step now. I'll—"

Tracker leapt to his feet, grabbed PJ by the collar, and shoved him down the tunnel. "Just run!"

They all ran as bugs poured out into the tunnel. They jumped, squashed, and shouldered their way through insects of all shapes and sizes until they were covered with them. PJ felt them writhing in his hair, tumbling down his shirt, squirming up his pant leg. He didn't have time to slap at the small ones, because he was too busy batting away the largest ones with the nastiest-looking stingers.

"There!" Tracker cried.

PJ saw a dim light at the end of the tunnel. He lowered his head and plowed through the swarming insects, feet crunching along the tunnel floor.

Suddenly, the tunnel opening was darkened by a huge shadow. A massive insect the size of a Volkswagen loomed over the exit. Bree, Tracker, and Toady all slowed, hesitating, but PJ charged ahead.

"No!" Tracker yelled.

"Wait!" Bree said.

PJ didn't hear them. He burst from the tunnel right beneath the monster bug. It reared up, and PJ dove to his left, rolling up against a boulder. The bug lunged, but the vicious swipe of its fierce-looking stinger fell short. PJ was out of range.

He looked down and grinned. "C'mon!" he shouted. "It's tied up!" Indeed, the monster insect was roped to a huge stake and couldn't reach him.

Tracker, Bree, and Toady burst out of the tunnel, beating off swarms of small bugs and a couple of large ones. "Get down and roll," Tracker barked. They threw themselves onto the stone floor, squashing, squishing, crunching, and mushing hundreds of bugs. All four of them twisted on the ground for a time, then rose slowly, swatting at the last clinging insects. They were all covered in bug guts of various colors.

PJ glanced at his three companions. "Gross," he said.

Tracker turned and began to examine the giant bug and its tether from just past the creature's reach. He was dripping bug juice, but didn't seem too bothered by it. "This is a goblin snare," he observed. "Another trick they learned from humans. They trap the bugs to eat, and for other sadistic purposes, it is rumored."

Bree wiped bug parts from her face and spat out a large moth.

PJ waved at the others. "Hey, isn't anyone else a little nervous about sticking around this tunnel?"

The giant insect surged forward, but the tether held. PJ stumbled backward.

Tracker didn't even flinch. "Relax. They don't come out into the open unless they act together. In the bug world, size matters, and their largest is all tied up at the moment. Without a giant leader to follow, they won't go any farther than the spot where this one is stuck."

Toady looked at PJ. "You ran right at it," he said. "You are indeed a brave warrior."

"Nah," PJ said. "I just screwed up so bad going into the tunnel I had to make up for it on the way out."

"He's right," Bree said. "Don't be impressed because he got us out of the trouble that he got us into." She stepped up to PJ. "And that's the last time I let you jeopardize this mission."

"Yeah?" PJ said. "What are you gonna do, kick me off the team?"

Tracker grabbed each of them by the shoulder. "Wait, you two," he said, pointing across the cavern. "There it is. . . . Argh."

33
THE SPLEECH

Sam's dad had once given him some advice about being backed into a corner. He'd told Sam that if anyone ever picked on him, he should hit them first. Of course, his father had been drunk when he said it, and every one of his dad's fights had landed him in jail or the hospital. But his dad had been adamant about sticking up for oneself, and it was the only advice Sam had ever gotten on the subject.

Sam gripped the stone rod hard as he watched for movement on the ceiling. He named the thing a "spleech," short for spider-leech, but he imagined the name would only stick for as long as it took the thing to track him down and deal him some horrible death.

Something twitched in the shadows above him. He gathered himself, and when he saw a spindly leg flick out into the light, Sam swung the pole upward as hard as he could.

The loop of rope at the end of the pole snapped around the leg, and Sam yanked the pole down. Sam felt a great weight resist his pull for a moment, then something came loose. The bloated body of the spleech plummeted from the darkness above and hit the ground next to him with a heavy *splat*.

The thing staggered to its many legs, rocking back and forth, stunned. Sam retreated, edging backward past a few more pens, and the dizzy thing lurched after him. Sam still had it hooked by the leg with the snare pole. He shoved the pole instinctively, and it stopped cold. With its leg still lassoed, it could come no closer than the length of the pole. Sam continued to back up as he held the spleech at bay. It gnashed its circle of triangular teeth and flailed with its sticklike limbs, but managed only to tear Sam's sleeve with one of its viciously serrated legs. They began a jerky, awkward dance, with the bug shoving forward and Sam shoving back with the stone rod.

At least it's not smart, Sam thought as he risked looking around to get his bearings. Sam saw animal pens off to each side of him. Big pens. Just then, the creature turned its attention to the pole, bringing its forelegs down upon it. *Crack!* Sam winced as the pole began to splinter in his hand. The creature began to pound the stone rod repeatedly with its full weight. *Crack-crack-crack!*

The pole buckled. There was no time to run away. Sam threw it aside and dove into the nearest pen.

34
ARGH

Hidden among the scattered rocks beyond the bug tunnel, PJ, Tracker, Bree, and Toady found themselves overlooking a huge cavern. At the center of the cave was a gigantic tumble of boulders.

At first PJ thought the sprawling mass of stone below was merely a towering rock formation gone awry, but as he stared harder, the contours and lines of a huge fortress slowly revealed themselves, and once he saw it, he couldn't understand how he'd missed it.

The goblin city of Argh was part rock formations and part bizarre stonework add-ons, which loomed and lurched darkly in all directions. Towers began to reach upward, then stopped before they went anywhere. Square bridges spanned nothing and quit halfway. Ground structures had gaps in their walls with neither rhyme nor reason to their location. There was no obvious main gate. In fact, the wide path that wound through the cavern toward the massive thing led to a blank wall with no visible access.

"Holy Frank Lloyd Wright!" PJ gasped. "That looks like Doctor Seuss's architect threw up."

"Doctor who?" Toady asked.

Tracker frowned, grim. "Behold Argh. 'Tis a great ugliness that mars the beauty of UnderEarth, a grim castle of stone held in the iron grip of the heir to the Great Goblin's throne, General Eww-yuk."

"Heavy," PJ said.

Bree pointed at the goblin city. "We will breach the wall at that low spot. Toady, you stay here." She motioned to Tracker and PJ. "You two follow me."

"Whoa, no breaching for me," PJ said.

Bree stared, puzzled.

"I don't breach," he repeated.

Bree threw her hands up, exasperated. "You don't *do* anything!"

"Look, you're the friggin' guardians," he said. "I'm just along for the ride."

Bree looked so frustrated that, for a moment, PJ thought she was going to punch him. Tracker put a hand on her shoulder. "Let it go, Brianna," he said. "Commitment, security, and responsibility are our guiding principles, but not necessarily those of an upworlder." He turned to PJ. "PJ, we will probably die today. You may join us or not."

"You make it sound so tempting," PJ said.

"We cannot make you come," Tracker continued. "As with all crossroads in life, there is always a choice to make, and this choice is yours alone."

They waited for PJ's answer. He glanced from Bree to Tracker. He studied the scars of many battles on Tracker's hands, the lines of many years in his face, and a determination in his expression that betrayed no regrets.

Bree already had some scars too. No lines, yet, but they would come now that she was the leader. The same look of determination haunted her features. They had purpose, both of them, something PJ had never found, never sought at all, really. But what sort of sense did rushing into the goblin stronghold make for him? *None*, PJ thought, *that's what sort.*

Finally, he shook his head. Toady looked up at PJ. "You're not going in?"

"Uhhh, no," PJ mumbled, "I'm not."

Toady's face fell. PJ glanced at Tracker. "But what about the kid?"

"What about him?" Bree said.

"I'm just worried. That's all. You said they skin, tenderize, and chop humans. I'd hate to think . . ." PJ couldn't finish the thought. "You'll look for him, right?"

"If we come across your brother, I will send him out with Bree," Tracker said. "I am not likely to come back."

"What are you talking about?" PJ said. "You pop in, grab the kid and the fireworks, kick some goblin butt, and pop back out. No problemo for an expert swordsman like you, eh?"

Tracker grinned. "You do have spirit. Don't let anyone tell you that you don't, including yourself. Good-bye, PJ. Good-bye, Toady." Tracker nodded at each of them and began his climb down the rocks.

Bree drew her sword. "My primary mission is to recover the explosives. If I come across your brother, I'll bring him out with me. But if you are really worried about him, you'll go in and get him yourself." Then she too scrambled over the rocks and started down the slope.

PJ and Toady watched Bree and Tracker climb down and break from the rocks toward a low point in the fortress wall, where they shimmied up without a rope.

"Oh, man," PJ said, almost to himself, "they're not really looking for the kid."

"A single life does not outweigh our entire mission," Toady said.

"Then it's a pretty crappy mission," PJ snapped back.

"Our mission is to keep the goblins from obtaining dangerous technology and access to the surface so we can prevent an interspecies war. What's yours?"

"I was supposed to watch Sam," PJ said.

35
THE BUG STABLES

Sam tumbled into the pen and rolled to his feet, grabbing a fist-sized stone. The spleech snapped the goblin snare pole in half and burst through the gate. Sam swung the rock and smashed the pursuing bug in the head, stunning it momentarily, then whirled around, looking for an escape or a place to hide.

He gasped. In the pen with him was another insect, one that reared up and towered over him, staring down with . . . recognition.

"Cheep!" chirped the huge insect.

Sam stared. "It's you!" The massive bug whose life he'd spared in the arena stood before him.

The spleech squealed with rage behind him. "Quick," Sam yelled, leaping across the pen toward the giant insect, "let me get behind you." But it ducked away, curling into a huge ball so that Sam could not get past. Sam rolled his eyes. "No, you big dope. I'm not attacking. Just let me hide!" The bug peeked out at him from where its head was buried under its tail.

Sam glanced back. His pursuer had recovered. It was frothing at the mouth and steadying itself on its multiple legs. Sam panicked. "Cheep!" he yelled at the huge, reluctant insect in the corner.

It raised its head. "Cheep?"

"Cheep! Cheep!" Sam screeched, trying desperately to imitate its voice, hoping to somehow get it to move.

The insect uncurled from its protective position. Sam backed against the larger bug as the grotesque eating machine came at him, its round mouth opening so wide that Sam could see down its gullet. To his disgust, he could see a stew of saliva and partially digested bug parts in the back of its throat. *Please don't let that be the last thing I ever see,* he thought.

The spleech rose up to loom over Sam and deal him a crushing blow beneath its ponderous body. Sam opened his mouth to scream. But instead of falling on top of him, the spleech continued rising upward.

"Cheep!" the giant bug behind Sam barked as it grabbed and lifted the spleech with its massive forelegs. It handled the obese bug easily, like a toy. "Cheep," it barked again, tossing the fat thing head over tail past Sam and out of the pen.

Sam hurried to the pen wall and looked over to see the spleech fleeing into the shadows. He took a deep breath and turned to his massive bug ally. "You saved me!" he exclaimed. "Thanks . . . Cheep."

The bug bobbed its head like a panting dog. It gazed squarely at Sam with its clear, bulging eyes, and Sam could have sworn it looked happy. "Cheep!" it replied.

36
LOOKOUT!

PJ and Toady watched from the nearby hill as Bree and Tracker reached the top of Argh's outer wall. As soon as they disappeared over it, a boulder at the base of the wall uncurled into a furry form and began to follow them.

"A goblin lookout!" Toady gasped. The goblin had tucked itself so tightly into a ball that its gray fur had lain flat like a stone surface.

"Oh, no!" PJ said. "What do we do?"

Toady could only shake his head. "There's nothing I can do. I've sworn to carry the news back to the rest, good or bad."

"But if we can head off that lookout, they still have a chance."

"It's no use. I can't risk going in. I must live. That is my vow." Toady stiffened his young upper lip. "I have a dire message to deliver to our last few survivors—we've lost our wisest soldier and most courageous leader, and the goblins still have the explosives."

PJ and Toady stared together, watching the goblin scout pick its way among the rocks, sniffing after Bree and Tracker. It only had to alert one of the goblins patrolling the walls above, and it would be over for the two brave guardians.

"Come," Toady said, rising to leave, "we must go."

PJ didn't move. "Oh, man, this is, uh . . . kinda my fault."

"No," Toady said. "We were foolish to think you were a heroic guardian warrior here to help us. It's not your fault. We were wrong to expect anything from you."

Toady waited for PJ to flee with him. PJ didn't move. "Go ahead," he said.

"What?" Toady said.

"I'll catch up, somehow." PJ stepped out from behind the rocks and started down the hill toward Argh.

"Are you sure?" Toady hesitated.

"Go on, get out of here, kid."

Toady's face brightened, and he turned to go.

"But, hey," PJ called after him before continuing down the hill, "since you're a messenger and all, if I don't make it back, could you tell the rest of the gang that I . . . I'm not a chicken." With that, PJ headed for the stronghold, stumbling his way down the steep slope.

Toady watched PJ go, pleased, proud, and slightly puzzled. "A chicken . . . ?"

Moments later, PJ approached the wall. The goblin lookout had sniffed out the spot on the wall where Bree and Tracker had gone over.

PJ took a deep breath. "He wasn't a chicken," he repeated to himself. "That's what my friggin' gravestone's gonna read." He stepped out from behind the rocks and walked straight toward the lookout. "Eh," he sighed, "I've heard worse." Waving at the goblin scout, he called out, "Hey! Hey, turd with legs!"

The goblin turned, surprised. "Arrrgh?"

"I'm here to see Mr. Yuck," PJ barked at the bewildered creature, "and I've got an appointment. Could you kindly direct me to his office?"

The lookout pulled a huge, jagged dagger from a leather sheath across its chest. PJ instinctively pulled the tiny knife Whitey had given him. It looked ridiculous compared to the heavy blade the goblin held in its furry fist. PJ looked down at his weapon, frowned, and put it away. "Okay, let's not decide this by who has the bigger weapon, huh? Just let me talk to Yucky. Let him decide what to do with me, eh?"

The lookout continued toward him, large dagger held high. PJ looked around for somewhere to run in case his negotiations failed, but he couldn't climb back up the steep, boulder-strewn hill faster than a goblin.

The lookout kept coming, so PJ kept talking. "You don't want to kill me," he cooed gently, as though trying to hypnotize it. The goblin did not slow.

PJ backed against a boulder. The thick, rough-edged dagger looked very painful. PJ put his hands up in a last-ditch attempt to surrender. "I mean, you don't want Yucko to find out that you killed his chance to learn about a new gadget, do you?"

37
BREE AND TRACKER SPLIT UP

Bree and Tracker dropped into the goblin city. The floor inside the wall was littered with tunnel entrances. It looked like a beehive. They ran and dove into the nearest opening to minimize the risk of being seen, then moved quickly, creeping from tunnel to tunnel. Tracker made decisions without hesitation. He had an uncanny sense of direction, and because the goblins had learned to tunnel from ants and termites, there was some order to the interior of the stone structure. "This way," Tracker mumbled over his shoulder to Bree, never looking back, "now this way, now here . . ."

Finally, he paused. He stopped so abruptly, in fact, that Bree almost ran into him. "Wait," he said. "Good fortune cannot account for the fact that we have not seen a single goblin in all of these halls."

"What does it mean?" Bree asked.

"They would not have all left the city," Tracker said. "They must be gathered somewhere."

As if in answer to the riddle, the bell clanged somewhere deep in the tunnels. Tracker stood motionless, listening until the sound faded away. Distant, muffled footsteps followed.

"That was our bell!" Bree exclaimed.

Tracker shushed her with a gesture and concentrated, evaluating the faintest echoes, estimating the distance, counting the number of feet. His decades in the caverns and tunnels of UnderEarth told him all he needed to know to decipher the meaning of even absolute stillness.

Finally, he turned to her. "They're all moving away from us. They've been summoned somewhere across the city. Our luck is excellent. While they are elsewhere, we can search this area for the explosives . . . and the boy."

Bree nodded, and Tracker motioned her into a larger corridor. They'd previously stuck to small passages, but now they ventured into a major goblin thoroughfare.

Soon they came within sight of a pair of huge double doors. A large goblin stood next to them, leaning on a crude partisan—a long stone spear whose spade-shaped tip curled out into points like a fishhook, perfect for gutting anyone within six feet.

"A guard," Tracker whispered to Bree. "We have come to an important area. Those doors are very ornate for goblins, and a soldier on watch here instead of off with the rest means it must be a very important room. I'll need to check inside."

Bree laid a hand on her bow. "I will take the guard," she said.

Tracker put a hand up to stop her. "Wait. It might raise an alarm if you do not kill it instantly. And there may be no need to kill if you are smarter than it . . . yes?"

"I'm smarter than a goblin," she snapped.

"Time for you to show it, my young leader." Tracker winked. "Get the guard away from the door, then forget about me and move on. We'll have twice the chance of finding what we seek if we separate."

Bree thought for a moment, then she removed her sword and bow and handed them to Tracker. She twirled a length of rope around her wrists, while Tracker grabbed the weapons with a nod. She took a deep breath and dashed from her hiding place.

Pretending to be an escaped captive, Bree raced past the guard and stumbled, falling unarmed and apparently bound at the wrists onto the floor of the tunnel. The surprised goblin lowered its weapon into thrusting position and stepped forward instinctively, taking the bait. Bree crouched, waiting for it to leave the door unattended.

The guard eyed her, eager but unsure. It glanced about before it moved any farther, unwilling to leave its post entirely. But a helpless human on the ground in front of it was almost too much to resist. Bree grabbed her leg and winced in fake pain, hamming it up.

The goblin grinned and trundled away from the door, coming straight at her. As it approached, she suddenly rose and limped off down the hall. It grunted and hurried after her. Bree jogged a little more quickly, just fast enough to stay a few steps ahead of the lumbering guard and its long, unwieldy weapon.

As the goblin followed Bree, Tracker slid from the darkness behind it. He hurried to the doors and put his shoulder against one thick rock slab. It swung smoothly on massive, well-worn stone hinges, and he slipped inside, pulling the door closed behind him.

Tracker turned and found himself in a great hall. Rows of crooked pillars lined each side of the massive room. They towered thirty feet high before widening to meet one another at odd angles on the pitted ceiling. The central aisle spread in front of Tracker nearly ten feet wide, and it was so long that he could just barely make out a grand stone chair atop the dais at its far end. His eyes were still sharp, though, even at his age, and he could see that there was something sitting on the throne.

38
EWW-YUK TAKES A MEETING

After the unsatisfying events in the arena, Eww-yuk had returned to his hall and amused himself by testing the human bell on his goblin soldiers. They learned quickly. Each time he rang it, every goblin within earshot rushed to the armory to grab a weapon in preparation for battle. Of course, there was no battle, and each time Eww-yuk saw their panicked faces, he'd enjoyed a good laugh.

Now he sat at his stone table sharpening his shiny-smooth tusks with a crude file. Brains stood before him, gesticulating toward a slate covered with diagrams of Sam's tennis shoe. Eww-yuk grunted and occasionally belched as Brains presented his findings.

"The top of the foot armor is dead animal skin," Brains said. "But the bottom is more interrrrresting. It is made from an unknown thing that I call 'boing.'"

"Boing?" Eww-yuk frowned.

"Yes, the boing is strong but bendy, and it bounces." Brains bounced the shoe on a nearby stone. "You see . . . boi-oi-oinggggg." Brains smiled and did it once more. "Boi-oi-oinggg!" The little goblin watched the shoe bounce, fascinated all over again. He did it yet again, and again. "Boi-oi-oingggg! Boi-oinggg! Boi-oi-oi-oi-oinggg!"

"I see!" Eww-yuk barked finally. "But what good is it to me?"

Brains gathered himself and the shoe. "If our soldiers had boing," he explained, "they could cross the flesh-eating grass without having their toes eaten."

"Ah, and soldiers with toes might serve me better than soldiers with no toes. I like the way you think. How do we make this boing?"

"I do not know yet."

"Arrgh," barked Eww-yuk, kicking over the slate of diagrams. "Come back when you are useful!"

Just then, the goblin lookout barged in, dragging PJ by the collar.

"Arrrrgh!" Eww-yuk growled. "What's this?"

The lookout pushed PJ onto the stone floor in front of Eww-yuk's chair. "It says it has a 'pointment," the lookout said. "I'm not sure what that is, but it sounds like 'impor-tant.'"

Brains hustled to Eww-yuk's ear, whispering so excit-edly that his words were jumbled and Eww-yuk had to slap him across the head to get him to make sense. "He is dressed like the boy," Brains managed finally. "Look at his feet . . . more boing!"

Eww-yuk nodded and waved the lookout away. "Good work. Your stupidity is exceeded only by your blind loyalty."

"Thank you, General," the lookout said, grinning. "But there was something else I was going to tell you. . . ." The goblin scout wrinkled its brow and thought hard.

"No, there wasn't," PJ said.

"No?" asked the lookout. "Because I remember that—"

"No, you don't," PJ said, interrupting the scout's derailed train of thought.

The lookout shrugged, bowed to Eww-yuk, and exited.

Eww-yuk gazed down at PJ, curious. "So, human, you have an appointment with me? This should be interesting, as I don't recall *ever* having had an appointment with a human."

"You sound like an intelligent goblin," PJ said.

"Yes. I talk good. I am General Eww-yuk, next to stand in line behind the Great Goblin."

"Do you mean next in line to *be* the Great Goblin?"

"I mean whatever makes me ruler when the Great One dies," Eww-yuk growled, annoyed.

"Then obviously I've come to the right place," PJ said. He took a deep breath and stood up to look Eww-yuk straight in his pale yellow eyes. "I've got a proposition for you, Yukker."

Eww-yuk cocked a furry eyebrow. "I suppose it includes me not having you gutted and turned on a spit over hot coals for lying your way in here."

"Uh, yeah . . . for starters. Anyway, I'm looking for this lost kid. Maybe you've seen him. He's about yay-high." PJ held out his hand palm-down near his chest. "He'd be dressed in a reasonably cool black concert T-shirt and sneakers."

Brains listened intently and murmured to himself. "Sneakers? Hmmmm."

"Can't be too many folks that fit that description around here, right?"

Eww-yuk stroked his fur, thinking. "And, if I have seen this 'kid' . . . ?"

"Well, you, uh, fellas like new gadgets, right?" PJ said.

"Gadgets?" Eww-yuk perked up.

Brains hopped over to Eww-yuk and whispered frantically in the larger goblin's ear.

Eww-yuk's yellow eyes flashed. "Ah, yes, gadgets! We like gadgets very much! Have you got a gadget?"

"Not on me, no," PJ said carefully, "but I know someone who might know where there are some, and I can show you how they work."

"What sort? Will they help me to climb?" Eww-yuk unfolded from his seat and rose, coming at PJ. "Do they make far things look closer? Tell me, tell me, tell me!"

PJ put his hands up, motioning for Eww-yuk to stop. "Whoa-ho-ho, slow down there, dude. Have you got the kid?"

"Yes, yes, of course," Eww-yuk said. "I have the human child. Now tell me! Show me! Show and tell!"

Brains shifted from foot to foot behind Eww-yuk, just as excited to learn something new.

"Prove you have him," PJ demanded.

Eww-yuk snapped his fingers at Brains, who quickly produced Sam's sneaker. PJ stepped toward it for a better look, but Brains huddled his arms around it, guarding it jealously.

It didn't matter. The odds of the goblins having more

than one pair of kids' shoes were remote. "You didn't tenderize him, did you?" PJ asked.

"I know *I* didn't," Eww-yuk said, glancing at Brains.
Brains shook his head.

"Okay, here's the deal," PJ said. "I hook you up with
this sweet gadget, and you slide me the kid. Copacetic?"

Eww-yuk looked to Brains for a translation. Brains just
shrugged. Eww-yuk took a guess. "You want to trade?"

"Bingo," PJ said. "You got it."

Eww-yuk clapped, delighted that he'd guessed right.
"And you want us not to eat you?" he clarified.

"That would have to be part of it, yes," PJ said. "Fact is,
I'd want you to let us go."

Eww-yuk consulted with Brains. They snarled and
growled at each other at length while PJ glanced about nervously, counting the number of guards in the room. He
was up to ten when Eww-yuk looked back up at him.

"It is a bargain." Eww-yuk smiled unpleasantly. "Brains,
see if we have eaten the child yet. Now, human, tell me
what you know."

"Well, there's this Slurpy guy," PJ began, "and he . . ."

39
BREE GETS DIRECTIONS

Bree trotted down the tunnel away from the pursuing goblin guard, slowing occasionally to give it the impression that it might catch her at any moment. It kept following her, but soon it was clear that it would eventually tire of the chase and simply raise the alarm. She came to a stone pillar and ducked behind it.

"Argh!" The goblin grinned. "I see you there, human. Come out or be skewered where you hide."

"Come get me," Bree taunted, sticking her head out from one side.

The guard thrust its wickedly sharp partisan at her. Only her catlike reflexes saved her from getting stuck. The weapon's metal tip clanged off the wall behind the pillar.

"A poor strike," she taunted, poking her head out on the other side. "Care to try again?"

It did. The goblin whipped the long rod around and swung it at her horizontally from the other direction. *Whangg!* This time the shaft of the weapon slammed against the side of the pillar. Again she ducked away a split second before one of the winged points of the partisan could bury itself in her head.

"If you can't capture an unarmed human by yourself, your friends will wonder if you are fit to guard that room full of . . . what is it, food?"

"Arrgh! I was not chosen to guard mere food. I am Thick, the Great Goblin's personal sentry."

Bree gasped. "The Great Goblin's chambers?"

"Of course. And if you are lucky, you'll be served there . . . as a meal. Now, come out from behind there."

"Oh, no." Bree frowned. "Tracker." But she didn't have time to go back.

Just then, the goblin guard lunged forward and reached around the pillar with both arms. Bree dodged backward and grabbed each of its furry wrists. True to its name, the goblin's arms were as thick as tree branches, but with a quick flex of her own arms, Bree slid the rope she carried off her wrists and over the goblin's paws. She yanked it tight and whirled the ends into a quick knot, tying the goblin's arms together behind the column.

"Argh! What's this?" The guard reared back, but it was stuck. "Arrrrrrgh!"

"Quiet!" ordered Bree, stepping out from behind the pillar. "Or else I will have to quiet you." She whipped out her dagger. The guard fell silent. It tugged at the rope, but it was no use.

"I need to know where the goblin called Brains keeps his gadgets."

The guard just frowned at her, angry and embarrassed.

"Come, come," she encouraged, "I don't have time to

wait, and I am still deciding how to best keep you quiet after I leave. I could cut out your tongue. . . ."

The goblin's bulging eyes widened even further.

"Or you could help me decide to do something less severe."

"That way," the guard mumbled. It pointed with one of its stocky legs and began to give directions: "Left Y tunnel, straight tunnel, third opening in first cavern, drop through the floor, and look for a door in the wall that you cannot see."

"A door I can't see?"

"You are a human," it said matter-of-factly. "You cannot read rock like a goblin. You might find it, you might not. But it will not be my fault if you don't," it added quickly.

Bree nodded. "Stick out your tongue." The guard cringed. Bree put the knife to its belly. "Do it," she growled.

Moments later, Bree scrambled down the hall in the direction the goblin had told her to go. It was probably not lying. It had neither the time nor intelligence to think up a good lie. And it would not cry for help, because she had tied its long tongue around its ear.

40
THE GUARDIANS

Braun led the young guardians toward the wall through the muck and mire of the swamp shallows. He stuck to the fringe, taking the long way around to avoid the deep sink-holes where the sweeper lurked. The awful story of Whitey's last stand haunted the entire group, and even though they hiked along the very edge of the bog, the youngsters glanced about wide-eyed, looking over their shoulders for any sign of the monster.

Braun was in no hurry to engage the goblins. With only twenty teen soldiers, even if they surprised the enemy, their odds were not good. Ten of the kids had swords, five were bowmen, and five others carried long spears. Most of them were too young for battle, but everyone would fight now. According to Bree, more than fifty goblins manned the wall, all armed to the teeth.

Braun decided he'd wait as long as he could to see if they heard from Bree and Tracker before they tried to sneak over the wall. Every soldier would count, and Bree and Tracker were the best they had left.

Soon the swamp ended and they were a comfortable distance from the sinkholes. Braun signaled his party to stop.

"We will make camp here. The wall is only a short march away now." He drew an hourglass from his pack. "If there is no word by the time the glass has been turned twice, we must go on and mount a final attack. We will try to climb the wall and surprise them." He took a deep breath. "I hope that, before then, we hear news from Toady."

As his fellows made camp, Toady tiptoed through the maze of antennae in the bug tunnel. It was the only path back that he knew. He looked left and right in the darkness. The walk was terrifying, especially after his first experience, but PJ's bravery had inspired him. "Steady . . . steady . . . ," he told himself.

Toady ducked a hanging web and dodged a sweeping antenna. As long as he didn't touch anything, he thought, he'd be all right. The path ahead was backlit by the distant glow at the far opening of the tunnel. To his relief, he didn't see any bug silhouettes. It seemed they didn't come out of their holes unless they were disturbed.

Toady reached a wide spot in the tunnel that he hadn't noticed on his first trip through—he'd been running too fast. He judged that he was about halfway and smiled, encouraged, until he heard a noise skittering behind him. Toady froze. There was skittering in front too. A horrible thought struck him—he was at the point in the tunnel farthest from the safety of either exit. Clever predators often waited until their prey were most helpless before attacking. Suddenly, it wasn't so comforting that no bugs had come out earlier. Shadows moved, and his heart sank as the cir-

cle of light at the end of the tunnel filled with dark writhing shapes. The bugs were out now, and he'd been caught
in their simple trap.

Something pressed against the top of his head, stroking
his hair in the blackness. He jerked away, and a large
shadow shifted above him. There was more scratching and
slithering all around him. Tiny feet skittered over one bare
hand. His foot bumped against a mushy lump that scuttled
away. He felt the soft, familiar brush of a searching antenna across his face. "Oh, no," Toady breathed, "not
again." Then he was yanked off his feet.

41
GADGETS

Three of Eww-yuk's largest guards barged into Slurp's sleeping cave. Slurp was still curled up under the bed ledge. He'd blended into the rock, nearly invisible, but they knew he was there.

"Argh," said the first guard, "come with us, Captain. The general wants to see you."

Slurp's yellow eyes shot open, alert. They shined in the dark hole like a pair of gold coins.

"Bring your things," the guard advised, "*all* your things."

Slurp uncoiled himself and emerged from the hole, straightening his armor and pulling his cloak carefully over the backpack he held concealed from the guards in the small of his back. He'd been asleep for some time, a much-needed rest. Now he stood and towered proudly over the largest of Eww-yuk's soldiers.

One of the guards quickly searched the hole and found nothing. The other two waited nervously, their furry fingers hovering near their weapons, but they didn't dare touch the huge goblin captain. Slurp sized up the guards and nodded, satisfied. "So he had to send three of you for me, eh?"

The guards entered Eww-yuk's hall with Slurp, one walking ahead of him and two behind. Eww-yuk sat in his chair. Seven more big goblins stood nearby. One held PJ by the shoulder.

"Argh!" Slurp snapped, glaring at PJ. "What's this?"

Eww-yuk laughed. "Ar-ar-ar-argh. You tell me, Captain."

"A human, and a scrawny one at that," Slurp said.

"It says it knows you," Eww-yuk said.

"What?" Slurp shrugged off the guards, walked to PJ, and sniffed him. As he sniffed, he leaned to PJ's ear and whispered fiercely, saliva flying, "You fool. You're going to get us both killed."

"Say it, don't spray it," PJ whispered back.

Slurp turned to Eww-yuk. "No. It does not smell familiar."

"Human," Eww-yuk said, "is this the miserable wretch of a goblin that you told me about?"

PJ leaned to look at the side of Slurp's head. He pointed to the bald spot and burnt fur just above Slurp's ear. "Yep." He nodded. "I did his hair."

Eww-yuk turned to Slurp. "What would you say is your biggest problem, Slurp?"

"I'm a perfectionist?" Slurp tried.

"No! You're stupid!" Eww-yuk barked from atop his stone chair. "You thought you could trick me? You thought you could hide things from me? Me! Arggggh!"

"Argh!" Slurp shouted back.

Eww-yuk descended into goblin grunts, which Slurp answered with equally vicious snorts and snarls.

"Arrgh! Argh! Ar-ar-arrrrgh!"

"Arrgh, aaaaargh."

"Argh! Ar-ar-ghhh, argh."

"Arrgh, arghhh!"

PJ watched, thinking their monosyllabic language was odd, but it was even odder that he was beginning to understand some of what they were saying.

Finally, Slurp growled something that made Eww-yuk furious.

"ARRRGH!" Eww-yuk slammed his furry fist down so hard on his stone chair that rock chips flew in all directions. "Search him!"

Three guards leapt at Slurp. The first grabbed the captain's thick wrist, but Slurp whirled, twisted the guard's arm, and sent it flying into the stone wall, where it crumpled into a pile. Slurp backhanded the next guard in the face with his huge paw, dispatching it with a nasty crunch as one of its tusks snapped in half.

Everyone froze, amazed at Slurp's power and speed. The third guard stood alone against him now. It frowned, realizing it was outmatched.

"Don't flee," Slurp advised quietly. "Eww-yuk will have you killed if you run. If you attack, I will merely beat you senseless."

The smaller goblin nodded, thankful, and charged at

him. Slurp dodged its blow, caught the guard beneath one massive arm . . . and beat it senseless.

"Enough," Eww-yuk barked from his seat, looking a bit worried, and he motioned the other seven goblin guards into the fray. All seven hesitated, pointing and grunting at one another, none wanting to attack first.

"Clubs!" shouted Eww-yuk.

The guards drew weapons, thick staves of light, hard stone. Slurp reached for his sword, then decided against it and flung himself directly into their midst like a big, furry bowling ball.

Clubs rose and fell, guards flew, claws and teeth tore and gnashed. PJ watched three more guards go down before the great captain finally succumbed to their superior numbers and blunt weapons.

When they finally had him pinned on the ground, one of them came up holding the bag of fireworks. "No!" Slurp yelled from his prone position. He was bruised and battered, but the fight was still not out of him.

"Bring that bag over here," PJ said. "I'll, uhhh, show you how the gadgets work."

The goblin guard began to waddle over to PJ with the bag.

"Wait!" Slurp growled. "The human cannot be trusted with those."

"Eh?" Eww-yuk grinned, relaxed now that Slurp was being held down by four other goblins.

"If we give him crap, he will use them to blow all our fur clean off!" Slurp shouted.

The guard stopped, took one look at the burnt fur on Slurp's head, and tossed the bag away. Eww-yuk frowned, unwilling to retrieve the bag himself.

"Look what he did to me!" Slurp said, turning his bald spot toward Eww-yuk. "The roar of it, and the blinding light . . . horrible. The human was not even touching the thing when it slammed into my head like an avalanche."

PJ inched toward the discarded bag. "That's crazy talk. Somebody shut him up!"

Brains started jabbering away into Eww-yuk's ear like a buzzing little insect. Finally, Eww-yuk barked over the chatter. "Guards, bring the sack to me!"

"No!" PJ said. "You don't know how to—"

"Silence!" Eww-yuk pointed his dagger at a guard and then at the bag. The guard was more afraid of Eww-yuk than the bag and reluctantly pushed past PJ to scoop it up in one of its hairy paws. "You don't think that I am as stupid as Slurp, do you?" Eww-yuk continued.

PJ glared at Slurp. "I don't think that's possible."

Eww-yuk received the bag and dug around inside of it as Brains scrambled around the stone chair trying to catch a glimpse. The general pulled out a Sonic Atomic Sky Blaster.

"They're too dangerous," insisted Slurp. "Our kind is not ready for such grim weapons."

"Bah," sniffed Eww-yuk. "I can control these gadgets— I'm bigger than them." He pointed at PJ and Slurp. "Hang the human and the traitor in a cell while I try to think about all of this. Hang them together—they seem to like each other."

The guards bound Slurp's limbs and hauled him to his feet. PJ's guard shoved him over beside the goblin captain.

"Brains!" Eww-yuk barked. "Take these to your lab and find out how they work." Eww-yuk handed the bag to an ecstatic Brains, who rushed into a corner to sift through the fireworks.

"You cannot do this," Slurp rumbled, stepping as close to Eww-yuk as his captors would permit. "I am a captain, and you are not Great Goblin."

"Not yet." Eww-yuk leaned over and whispered privately to Slurp. "But soon, when the Great Goblin is gone, I will make you disappear . . . poof! Just like my stinky brothers."

"Yo!" PJ shouted over their growling. "What about our bargain?"

"You idiot," Slurp said. "You can't trust us—we lie."

"No way!" PJ yelled at Eww-yuk as the guards began to haul them off. "What kind of leader lies right in front of everyone?"

"Your kind," Eww-yuk said evenly. "Where do you think we learned it?"

42
THE GREAT GOBLIN

The Great Goblin sat on its throne at the far end of the huge cavern, bent and gnarled with age, but alert. It too had eyes that were better in their day, but they were still good enough to see that there was someone in his hall. "Hu-uuuuman," it rumbled.

The goblin's deep voice reverberated down the hall like a rolling wave, seeming to gain volume as it came at Tracker. He stood firm, unshaken. "Ho, Great Goblin," he replied boldly. "I am Thomas, known as Tracker, brother to Jonathan, known as Hunter, and son of Frederick, known as . . . Fred."

The Great Goblin frowned and thought hard. "Fred is dead. I saw to it myself long ago, at the Battle of the Black River."

Tracker's eyes narrowed.

"You are his offspring here to slay me, then, eh?" the goblin said.

Tracker had not come to assassinate the goblin leader, but the chance to avenge his father set his heart pounding. He drew his sword and started forward, easing directly down the center of the great hall.

The Great Goblin rose. Its skin creaked like stiff

GOBLINS!

leather, and internal parts of its anatomy sloshed about, but as it unfolded painfully from its massive throne, the source of its authority was apparent. Like Slurp and Eww-yuk, the Great Goblin was huge.

"You offer me a warrior's death," the old goblin said, "the way creatures like us should die, not sitting in a chair." It coughed and stretched its long limbs. "I welcome you . . . and offer you the same."

Tracker took a deep breath but kept his pace. He rubbed his own aging, aching back and adjusted his grip on his sword. The Great Goblin retrieved a spiked scepter from beside his throne and limped off the dais, walking down the aisle to meet Tracker.

They marched toward each other, each finding his step, and soon they were trotting. No alarm was raised, no more words were spoken, and neither showed any hint of doubt. Each kept both eyes locked on the other, and, finally, they began to run down the center of the great hall, weapons raised.

The aches and pains of many decades were ignored and faded like a memory as the two old soldiers reached deep into themselves to find their youth. They grinned, both of them, as they rediscovered the mighty warriors they once were and charged headlong into battle.

43
SAM IN THE LAB

The door out of the bug stables led into a low tunnel. Sam crept along with the giant insect Cheep following and trying in vain to hide its bulk behind the small boy.

"Keep quiet, Cheep," Sam said. "I think I hear something coming." It was unmistakable and growing louder— the sound of goblin feet padding toward them. Sam leaned against a recess in the wall, hoping to peek around the corner of the tunnel. Suddenly, the rock behind him shifted, revealing a crack in the shape of a door. He pushed on it. The rock slab swung inward, and he hurried inside. Cheep squeezed through the door behind him, desperate not to be left alone, and the door swung back into place behind the big bug.

Sam was already exploring the room. Stone bowls, rough metal spoons, and cups sat on flat rock tables. Crude hammers, tongs, and other hand implements were scattered around like toys dumped out of their toy box. A slate board on the wall was covered with drawings that looked like grappling hooks and ropes. Another crude drawing was unmistakable—Sam's tennis shoe.

"My shoe! This must be Brains's lab." Sam was unsure

why he was excited, but he was excited nonetheless. He hoped to find his sneakers. One of the ill-fitting sandals Slouch had furnished him was giving him a blister. He saw human clothing—empty robes, belts, and boots—piled ominously in one corner. His shoes were not in the pile, but there, on the top, was something else that belonged to him—his backpack.

"The fireworks!" he exclaimed. For some reason, finding the fireworks struck Sam as important. It was as though he'd recovered his original mistake, and if he ever got out, returning them would be the first thing he'd do.

When Sam lifted the fireworks from the pile where Brains had stacked them, he discovered other items underneath—a nylon rope, a rock hammer, coats, a plastic spork, and a three-pronged steel grappling hook with a stamped label that said BELLINGHAM OUTFITTERS, an outdoor adventure store in the large town down the road from Sumas.

Oh, dude, Sam thought, *this is caver climbing gear!*

Sam took his backpack and quickly picked through the equipment. He found a discarded driver's license in the pile. The photo on it was the goofy-looking guy with a ponytail hanging in the meat room. *These dudes must have climbed down here through another hole.* Sam grimaced. *And the goblins must have . . . eaten them.*

He located a crumpled piece of paper in the pocket of an Eddie Bauer jacket. Rough sketches of tunnels and caves ran from the top of the paper to the bottom. Sam realized it was a hand-drawn map. The map ended with an interrupted half sketch of Argh. Sam traced backward from Argh to the upper edge of the page. The map's starting point was the surface. His heart did a flip-flop. *Another way out!*

44
SLURP ROCKS

The guards hung PJ by his arms in a cave and barred the door. Slurp hung on the other side of him.

"Argh," the captain growled to himself.

"What are you whining about?" PJ replied, "I had a simple plan. Get the kid, get the fireworks, light off a few, and run like heck. You messed it all up."

"Yes, I have failed." The mighty goblin hung limp, eyes downcast. PJ felt strangely sorry for him. He seemed like a proud beast—stupid, ugly, and he spit when he spoke, but proud. He had beaten three guards by himself and fought hard against the rest. Hanging defeated in chains seemed wrong for him.

"Don't feel bad," PJ said. "That was a pretty impressive bit of fightin' back there."

Slurp slumped. "I do not feel bad . . . I am empty of all feeling."

PJ decided to leave him alone, and they hung in silence for a time. But without conversation, hanging in the room with a toothy goblin felt creepier than before. PJ began humming to himself.

"What?" Slurp said.

"I didn't say nothin'," PJ said.

"But those sounds you're making, what are they?"

"Music?" PJ said. "Don't you have music?"

Slurp frowned. "What is it?"

PJ eyed his furry cellmate, curious. "Tap your foot."

Slurp looked suspicious.

"It's something new to learn," PJ offered, "maybe the coolest thing ever."

Even beaten and trussed in chains, Slurp couldn't resist the chance to learn something new. He gently tapped the stone floor. *Tap-tap-tap.*

PJ began to hum, following Slurp's cadence.

Slurp stopped suddenly. "Argh! What is that? It was just sounds at first, but then there was something else."

"It's rhythm," PJ said. "It can make you feel anything— happy or sad, mellow or jazzed, satisfied or frustrated—"

"I feel that!" Slurp blurted. "Frustrated."

"Stomp it out, my man," PJ said, "like you mean it."

Slurp stomped. *Boom-boom-bah . . . boom-boom-bah . . .*

PJ resumed humming.

After a moment, Slurp nodded, half grinning and de-lighted. "This gives me . . . energy."

"A good song can make you feel like you can do any-thing," PJ said. "Like maybe get us out of here? You're a leader-type dude, right?"

"You don't understand," Slurp replied. "I cannot be leader over Eww-yuk. I am from the Great Goblin's second litter. Eww-yuk is first litter and next in line for the throne. He is the only surviving pup of that original batch. The rest all vanished over a cliff when they were young."

"Man, that sounds pretty harsh."

"Yes. They all disappeared—my half brothers Rotty, Rank, Stank, Dank, and little Pew. Strangely, Eww-yuk was the only one who didn't fall." Slurp sighed. "Five of the furriest and most curious little goblin pups you ever saw. I can picture them looking over the edge, Eww-yuk grinning behind them. I can even hear him in my head—'Look down, go ahead. A little closer. A little closer.' Then they lean, and . . . with all of them packed together, it would have only taken a gentle nudge, and suddenly he is the only heir left alive."

"Can you prove that?"

Slurp thought hard for a moment. "I've always thought Eww-yuk had his paw in their disappearance," he said. "After what he said to me today in his hall, I am certain. But it doesn't matter. He is heir now. The only way for a goblin born into the second litter to become . . ."

"The big cheese?" PJ suggested.

"Right. The only way I become a big cheesy goblin is to defeat Eww-yuk in a fight to the death, just the two of us. But he is cunning, and I am not so smart as I might seem."

"No worries," PJ said. "You don't seem that smart. But I've been thinking. Y'know, Eww-yuk might be big, but I bet he's gotten soft sitting up here in this schizoid palace saying 'bring me this' and 'bring me that.' He's not out honing battle skills in the field, storming walls and fighting big, nasty sweeper slugs. Dollars to doughnuts he's been a couch potato ever since he got this desk job. You dig?"

Slurp merely gave him a blank look.

PJ tried again. "When's the last time he fought some-one without calling in his bodyguards?"

Slurp cocked his head, interested.

"I saw you fighting," PJ said. "You didn't send your goblins to do anything you wouldn't do yourself."

"Of course not," Slurp snapped.

"That's right. A guy who can step up and take his life by the reins instead of letting it pass him by can do any-thing."

"Like you." Slurp nodded.

PJ paused. "Uh, not so much."

"But you have been brave and clever to get in there," Slurp said. "And you make music. You must be well re-spected among humans."

PJ chuckled, then went silent for a moment. "No," he said finally, "you can't get people to respect you just by being clever once in a while. You need to come through when they are really counting on you."

"Arrgh . . . and I shall!" Slurp snarled. He began to stomp in rhythm.

"Whoa." PJ held up his hands. "Good energy. But I think we need a little reality check at this point. Remem-ber, we're in a dungeon, we got no weapons, we're chained up, and Yuck-yuck's too sly to agree to a game of one-on-one with you."

"Reality? Yes. Right. You are . . . a friend."

"Flattered."

"But I have many friends," Slurp said.

"Imaginary ones don't count," PJ replied.

"Many!" Slurp insisted.

"Calm yourself," PJ said. "I'm not saying people don't like you. I just don't see how that helps us right now."

Clang!

Just then the door swung open and a stocky goblin entered. It carried a large, sharp, curved tool the shape of a scythe. In the darkness of the cave, it looked like a squat stand-in for the Grim Reaper.

45
NOT SO DIFFERENT

In the echoing vastness of the great hall, Tracker and the Great Goblin raged through the stone columns, battling furiously.

Tracker's blade whirled, weaving a curtain of glittering steel through which it seemed nothing could penetrate. He circled his larger, slower opponent, probing its defenses with thrusts so quick they would have shamed the strike of a cobra.

But the Great Goblin's strength surprised him as it struck mighty blows again and again with its heavy scepter. Each swing pounded Tracker's sword away so that the aging human warrior had to stumble backward or leap aside to recover, and the clashing weapons sent the metallic song of battle ringing through the vast chamber.

Neither could land a solid blow upon the other's body. The Great Goblin could not corner Tracker, who danced and parried, always threatening with lightning jabs of his sharp weapon. Yet Tracker could get no closer to his goblin foe than the reach of its long arms and huge scepter. No delicate parry within the sweep of the heavy, blunt cudgel would stop it from smashing through to flesh and bone. They were very different fighters, but evenly matched.

The Great Goblin sounded no alarm, nor called for help. Tracker found it strange. The leader had only to cry out with a high-pitched goblin screech, and soldiers would almost certainly flood the room in moments. Tracker thought Bree. She had obviously taken care of the guard outside the door, because neither she nor the guard had come back to enter the fray. He was proud of her, and he silently wished her good luck, for he was fairly certain he would die as soon as a blow was landed on either side. Either the Great Goblin would kill him, or it would call for aid as soon as Tracker gained the upper hand. Unless, of course, he landed a blow that was instantly fatal.

They fought on the uneven steps of the Great Goblin's own throne now. Tracker dodged backward, stumbled, and the goblin was upon him. They clinched, grappling with their free arms, tangling legs, and flailing with their weapons. Tracker was caught in the sweep of the massive scepter's terrible swing, and the weapon fell upon his knee, destroying it with a sickening *crunch*. He staggered, and a second blow shattered his ribs. He went down and coughed blood.

The Great Goblin stood over him. "You will die from that," it said matter-of-factly.

Tracker nodded. "As will you," he said.

The Great Goblin looked down. Black fluid was pouring from a tidy slice in its furry stomach. Tracker had not bothered to parry the deadly blows dealt by the goblin. Instead, he'd struck his own blow—a quick, surgical flick of his wrist that sent the tip of his sword skimming through the thick flesh of the goblin lord's belly.

The Great Goblin shuffled to where Tracker lay slumped on the dais and fell into a sitting position beside him. Its body was thin now, weak, its vital fluids emptying out. Tracker was still breathing, but not well. Both were dying.

Tracker turned to the aging goblin. "My father is avenged," he said.

The goblin nodded, then replied, "Do you know who killed my father?"

"I believe it was my great-uncle," Tracker wheezed through his ruined lungs.

"Yes, and my cousin killed him," the Great Goblin grunted. "We are part of a long tradition of avengings, you and I. But I have sat on my throne puzzling over a question very much lately: Whose father killed whose father first?"

Tracker thought hard. "I don't know," he answered finally.

The goblin laughed, its empty chest rattling as death drew near. "Yes, I don't know too. I was hoping you could tell me."

Tracker allowed himself a pained grin. "Perhaps we are not so different," he said.

46
SLURP AND DRULE

PJ and Slurp hung together as the goblin with the scythe walked toward them. "Oh, gawwwd!" PJ cried. "They're here to skin, chop, and tenderize me!"

But the goblin ignored PJ and stepped up to Slurp instead, sniffing him. The stocky goblin smirked. "Hello, Slurp," it said.

"Drule," Slurp replied, "you are late."

"I got lost," replied Drule.

Slurp laughed. "Ar-ar-arrrgh . . . you idiot."

"Idiot, eh?" Drule frowned. "I'm not the one hanging from the ceiling."

Three smaller goblins rushed in and started working on Slurp's chains. Drule used the scythe to break the rock restraints. They worked quickly, and PJ marveled at their ability to make short work of their own goblin-made bonds. Suddenly, Slurp was free. Drule and the other goblins headed for the door, and Slurp began to follow.

"Uh, dude . . . ?" PJ called after him.

Slurp stopped and turned. "Argh?"

"Can you help out a fellow inmate here?"

Slurp turned to Drule. "I want to take it with me."

"Good idea," Drule said. "We'll need something to eat on the road."

Slurp turned to PJ. "Don't worry, Drule is from my litter." Slurp spoke to Drule. "Not to eat. He is my new . . . friend."

Drule stared. "He's a human."

Slurp frowned and looked at PJ. He examined him carefully, sniffed him, then feigned surprise. "Argh! You're right!" He descended into a series of goblin chuckles.

"What's wrong with you?" Drule said.

Slurp began to hum. PJ grinned and joined him.

"Stop that!" Drule snapped. "We must get out or Eww-yuk will have our heads on pikes."

"Yes," Slurp chuckled, "that sounds . . . uncomfortable."

"Hey," PJ interrupted, "what about me?"

Slurp pointed to PJ. "Come on, Drule, do not be so—"

"Uptight," PJ suggested.

"Yes," Slurp said, "do not be so uptight."

"Arrrrgh!" Drule growled.

"Argh, yourself," snapped Slurp. "Take it down!" The three smaller goblins hustled to snap PJ's shackles with their stone tools, and soon PJ was free.

"We must avoid other goblins," Drule hissed at Slurp. "Everyone knows you."

"Yes," Slurp said. "It's because I take life by its reins. Because they know I step up."

"It's because you're a captain," Drule grunted, "and you have a big burnt hole in your furry head."

PJ stood nearby as the goblins crouched by the door to the cell, listening for movement outside, their tall ears cocked forward. Drule leaned up next to Slurp.

"Why do you keep talking to it?" Drule grumbled.

"It gave me something," Slurp said.

Drule brightened, interested. "What? A cooking tool? A new type of weapon?"

"Something even better."

"What could be better than a weapon?"

"Confidence," Slurp said.

"Confidence?"

"Yes . . . strong, certain, and utterly false confidence."

"Hmmm." Drule nodded, trying to understand. "But you know that we must flee and never return."

"I will go back to my soldiers at the human fortress and face Eww-yuk there," Slurp said.

"Then you are as stupid as everyone says," Drule mumbled.

"Yes, I am!" Slurp growled. "But General Eww-yuk will not be Great Goblin while I still live, and if I fall, at least he will bear the full brunt of my stupidity before I die!"

PJ held his hand up to get Slurp's attention. "Listen, Slurpy," he said. "I need to get out of here, but there's something I gotta do before I go, so I think this is where we say adios." The goblins stared blankly. "I know you gotta meet your nemesis in mortal combat, fulfill your destiny, and blah, blah, blah, but I got my own problems. So once we get off death row here, you go one way, and I'm going the other. All right?"

Drule and his lackeys tensed for a confrontation and laid their paws on their weapons.

"And us being buddies now and all," PJ said carefully, "it would be cool if you'd let me leave without any trouble, okay?"

Slurp motioned Drule back. "It is cool." Slurp nodded.

"Cool," PJ confirmed. "You're my main man."

"My main man," Slurp repeated, grinning.

"Yep. But before I go, I'm gonna need directions out of beautiful downtown Argh, some climbing gear, and I really want to know where I can find a certain human kid. . . ."

47
BARGLE

Sam let Cheep lead the way. It wasn't easy—the giant bug kept trying to hide behind him, but he managed to push, shove, and cajole the thing into moving ahead. He figured that the insect must have a sense of smell or some sort of buggy instinct to follow that could find them a way out.

The next thing he knew, they were back in the meat room.

"Oh, man!" Sam complained. "We can't stay here." He pushed past a bug body that appeared to be an earthworm with a row of eyes lining its back. The eyes suddenly opened.

"Ahhh!" Sam yelped.

"Skreee!" Cheep screamed back.

The eyes fell closed, and the worm did not move again. The bug was dead. It was just a reflex action. Unfortunately, their own reflexes had been to yell loudly.

Footsteps sounded in the corridor outside the door. Sam and Cheep both froze. Someone or, more likely, some goblin was coming.

Sam ducked behind his giant bug friend. Cheep tried to hide too, but did so by taking hold of the ceiling and curling its huge body up into the air, leaving Sam standing alone among the slabs of meat and chilled bug carcasses.

The door to the meat room slid open. *Clank!* Sam couldn't see through all the bodies, but someone had definitely come into the room.

"Cheep?" whimpered the bug.

"Shush," Sam whispered. "We're trying to hide here."

A goblin voice oozed across the room. "Helloooo . . . hello? Are you back, little escapee snack?" Sam recognized the grotesquely lilting voice. It was the goblin Bargle.

"Oh, no," Sam whispered. "It's the hungry guy, and he's looking for me!"

To Sam's surprise, Cheep lowered its long body and wound into a protective ring around him, then fell motionless, playing dead.

Bargle navigated the meat room, peeking around bug bodies and ducking to look beneath them. "I hear, but don't see," he said. "Say something more, little snacky-snack." Bargle approached, pushing aside hanging meat. "Ah, now I smell. Yes, I smell live meat, meat so sweet, meat to eat."

Bargle followed his snuffling snout and eased up next to Cheep's huge body. He squatted and looked underneath, where he spied Sam's legs sticking out. He drew a dagger from his belt and reached down, aiming to cut a tasty strip of flesh from Sam's exposed calf.

Just then, Cheep thrashed. "Skreee!" The bug's tail whipped out and knocked Bargle onto his back. *Whump!*

Sam scrambled up on top of the unwound bug. Bargle

shook his thick head and crawled to his feet, ready to climb up after Sam. "Argggh! You cannot hide, snack!"

Sam glanced about. Bargle was right. There was no place to hide. Cheep's head was buried in its tail. Beyond its sudden spasm of fear, the bug was no help.

Bargle tucked his knife away in his thick fur and reached up to scale Cheep's shell.

Suddenly, a figure appeared in the doorway behind Bargle. "Leave the kid alone," the figure growled, "he ain't goblin grub."

Sam gasped. It was PJ!

Bargle turned. "What's this? Food that finds its own way into the pantry?" Rather than looking worried, the goblin seemed pleased at the prospect of more tender human meat. He reached for his knife and turned to deal with PJ.

Sam couldn't believe that PJ was actually standing there in the doorway. PJ was, frankly, one of the last things Sam had expected to see. *But it's not like he wandered down here by accident,* Sam thought. Clearly, PJ had come to rescue him.

PJ twirled a rope and grappling hook that Slurp had given him. He swung it at Bargle, and it flew right between the goblin's crooked ankles.

Bargle bent and looked back through his own bowed legs. "A miss! Ha-ha! You missed!" Bargle waved his dagger with maniacal glee.

PJ yanked the hook back. The hook caught Bargle's left leg and upended him. Bargle landed flat on his back again. *Whump!*

Bargle groaned and sat up just as Sam swung a slab of hanging bug meat toward him. *Whump!* Bargle was knocked flat yet again.

Sam put his weight behind another swinging slab, but Bargle'd had enough. He ducked and scrambled out the door past PJ. "Help! Help!" he cried as he ran away down the hall. "The food's gone bad! It fights! It fiiiiights!"

"PJ!" Sam shouted.

PJ hurried into the room toward Sam. "Kid! Kid! You okay?"

Sam ran to him. They met halfway and embraced for several seconds before the two boys simultaneously realized that they were too cool to be hugging. Each took a step back, and they stared at each other from the safe distance of just beyond arm's length, both grinning ear to ear.

"How'd you find me?" Sam blurted.

"Man, don't ask." PJ laughed, shaking his head. "I been looking all over for you." He couldn't help himself—he reached out to tousle Sam's hair. "I hate to say it, you little punk, but I'm actually really happy to see you."

"Yeah," Sam agreed, looking around, "normally I wouldn't hug another guy either. So where's your dad? Is the search party looking in other rooms?"

PJ frowned. "There's, umm, not really a search party."

"What?" Sam said.

"It's just me."

"Just you? But we're in the middle of a city full of goblins."

"A fact of which I am painfully aware," PJ said. "I had to let them catch me and toss me in a cell just to get into this place."

"That's not any smarter than what I did."

"I know," PJ sighed, "and when I have time, I'll start regretting it, but for now let's just make the best of things and get moving."

He stepped forward to take Sam's hand. Sam turned and tapped Cheep on the head. The giant bug rotated its eyes toward them.

PJ stopped in his tracks. "Whoa!"

Sam grabbed PJ's arm. "Can I keep him?"

"What?" PJ exclaimed, backing away. "No!"

"Why not?" Sam whined.

"For one, we have to get out of here. For two, that thing is, like, a giant praying mantis. And for three, because I said so!"

Sam looked up at PJ with pleading eyes. "But they'll kill him."

"We don't even know what it eats . . . maybe us."

"He just saved my life," Sam said. "I call him Cheep."

PJ looked up at the bug, then down at Sam. He sighed. "Cheep, huh?"

48
SLOUCH

Sam inched along through a pitch-black tunnel behind an unhappy PJ, who jumped every time the giant, nervous Cheep nestled up close to him for comfort.

"Where are we?" Sam asked.

"I don't know," PJ said. "That goblin we just thumped on went off screaming in the direction I was told to go. This is the only other way."

Suddenly, PJ and Sam stumbled out of the darkness into a well-lit, wide-open space. The empty area was surrounded by stone bleachers. "Uh-oh," Sam breathed. "The arena."

Cheep peeked out from behind them. "Cheep?" The bug sounded as concerned as Sam.

One of the gates used by the gladiators in battle was open nearby. A hunched figure shuffled out through it. Sam frowned, recognizing the dark creature, and a shiver ran down his spine. It was his goblin trainer, Slouch.

"Argh, my human and my insect. Welcome back, my two fighters. Ah, and you've brought another recruit! Goooood. I always like to add to my stable, both bug and human."

"Wait a minute," Sam said. "You owned both me and Cheep?"

"What's going on?" PJ whispered.

"I own all fighters." Slouch grinned. "The arena is my show."

"So you win no matter which one of us wins!"

"Ah, yes. Win-win. A position I like to be in. Come, I get you back to fighting. The crowd enjoys you." Slouch leered at Sam, his long, gnarled claws extending toward the boy.

"Hold it, bud!" PJ snapped. "I've come way too far for this kid to let some loser like you get your meat hooks in him." PJ stepped between Slouch and Sam as Cheep assumed his customary fetal position. PJ motioned Sam up onto Cheep.

Sam didn't want to sit the fight out. After their success in driving off Bargle, he wanted to help again. But the vantage point atop Cheep was the best in the arena. He threw his arms around one of Cheep's legs and clambered up.

"You think you can tell Slouch who is a loser, human?" Slouch sneered at PJ. "No, no. Slouch will tell you—a loser is one who tries but dies. Or worse, one who does not try at all." Slouch grinned and flexed his claws in and out like a cat.

PJ drew the tiny knife that Whitey gave him. "Keep your weapon up!" Sam shouted.

"Don't backseat duel for me, man," PJ said, but he followed Sam's advice, raising the knife over his forehead.

"Arrrrrgh," Slouch said, circling PJ.

PJ backed around the arena to keep space between him and the advancing goblin.

Sam watched from on top of Cheep, who shook with fear. There had to be something he could do to help, Sam thought. But what could he use as a weapon?

"PJ," Sam whispered suddenly, "lure him in close and give me the knife."

Slouch ignored Sam's whispers and lunged at PJ.

PJ ducked as Slouch's claw grazed his cheek. It was clear he couldn't outmaneuver the gladiator goblin. Eventually, Slouch would find a gap in his amateur defense and slash him viciously. PJ backed up toward Sam, shuffling and weaving until the old creature had pushed him into the corner formed by the wall and Cheep's curled body. "Argh, you are good, human. I see you learn from each move I make. I teach you to fight in the arena too, argh? Or you rather die now?"

PJ braced himself against the wall. Sam winked at him.

"No," PJ said, watching Slouch carefully. "I think we have something to teach you instead." PJ lowered his weapon.

Slouch grinned when he saw the weapon drop. He and his razor claws drew a step closer. "I am old. I have fought many matches and seen many more! What could you possibly teach me?"

As Slouch spoke, he lunged again, trying to take PJ by surprise. PJ, who appeared to have no plan, threw himself onto all fours on the ground and tossed the knife up to Sam.

Sam caught the knife and jabbed Cheep in the butt with it.

"Skreeee!" Cheep's body exploded from the fetal position. Its powerful tail uncoiled, snapping over PJ's head and scooping Slouch into the air like a golf ball. *Whupp!* The old goblin flew across the arena and into the stone seats.

Spppletch!

Dark goo sprayed across three rows of benches, and the goblin called Slouch, who'd sent countless humans, insects, and other unknown animals to their deaths, was no more.

PJ shook himself and rose from the ground.

"Teamwork," Sam called after Slouch, "that's what a couple of losers can teach you."

Cheep blinked, bewildered, and rubbed its abdomen with its forelegs. "Make that three losers." Sam patted the massive insect's shell near the wound. "Sorry, man . . . er, bug. It had to be done. You'll heal."

"Cheep?" Cheep glanced about. Now that the immediate danger had passed, the great insect took stock of their surroundings. Suddenly, Cheep cocked its head, climbed into the stands, and headed for the dark seats at the top of the arena.

Sam clung to Cheep's back. "Hey!"

"Where the heck are you two going?" PJ yelled after

them. He scaled the arena's half wall and chased his small and large companions up through the rows of benches.

"Cheep!" the bug squealed.

At the top of the bleachers, Sam suddenly saw why the giant insect had charged off. Over and beyond the wall, the arena opened to a cavern outside. "This is it!" Sam called back to PJ. "A way out of the city!"

PJ arrived and looked over the edge. It was ten stories straight down to the cave floor.

"I mean, it would be a way out," Sam added, frowning, "if we could fly."

PJ scowled at Cheep. "Briiiilliant, cockroach. No chance you've got wings under that exoskeleton, is there?"

Just then, a cluster of goblins burst into the arena. "This way! I still smell them!" Bargle led the small pack of soldiers toward the bleachers.

Cheep looked over the edge of the arena, then back at Sam and PJ expectantly. "Cheep!"

"What?" Sam snapped.

The goblins poured into the bleachers, scrambling over the rock seats toward them.

"Cheep!" squealed the bug.

"What?" PJ echoed.

Cheep gave up and disappeared over the wall.

"Cheep, no!" Sam yelled, lunging toward the precipice.

"He's gone, kid," PJ said, grabbing his arm. "Don't look."

"We have them!" Bargle shouted from below. Indeed,

the goblins were almost upon them. PJ didn't even bother to draw the small knife.

Suddenly, Cheep's head popped back up over the edge of the arena wall. "Cheeeeeep!" the bug screamed.

Sam looked down. Cheep's many legs clung to the sheer wall like suction cups. "Get on!" Sam yelled. He pulled PJ onto Cheep's back as goblins pounded up the steps, swinging axes and clubs. The two boys held their breath, and Cheep lurched back over the edge.

Moments later, Cheep was climbing down the vertical wall as Sam and PJ clung to its neck for dear life. The angry goblins stared after them from far above, unable to do more than hurl curses down at them.

"Wahoo!" Sam yelled.

PJ held on tight, his eyes mashed closed. "I'm not looking," he said. "You look for both of us, 'cause I'm definitely not looking!"

49
BREE GETS BRAINS

Bree scooted down the tunnel, eyes flitting about. She hadn't run into any goblins. Each time she heard them coming, a distant clanging bell summoned them away. But she knew that her luck wouldn't last forever, and she would not have much more time to search for the fireworks.

At last she came to the area the goblin guard had described as the tunnel to Brains's lab. Bree began to feel along the wall for fissures that might betray the door's location.

A murmuring sound floated down the hall toward her. A goblin mumbling to itself was coming her way.

Bree concentrated on the rock and found something that did not feel quite natural. She ran her hand over the spot, found a grip, and tugged. The stone door shifted, exposing its outline and a handle. She grabbed it and pulled. Nothing happened. The goblin drew closer. She drew her small dagger and put her back to the wall, waiting in ambush, but when she leaned against the door, it swung inward, and she tumbled into Brains's lab.

When Brains returned, he immediately knew something was wrong. He sniffed the air, then ran to his instruments. "Argh. Someone has been here!"

Above him, in the shadows of the ceiling, Bree clung to a rock outcropping like a human fly with her knife in her teeth and her rope over one shoulder.

Brains moved about the lab, fussing and fuming. Soon, he was directly beneath her. He sniffed the air again, suspicious, and when he looked up, Bree let go.

Whump!

She fell on top of him, and their bodies both hit the floor hard. Brains's furry, squishy bulk cushioned her impact some, and she hopped up quickly. A very small goblin, his strength was no greater than hers, and she wrestled him over so that she could force one knee onto his throat. With a few quick twists of her rope, she had him bound and gagged.

Bree rubbed her neck. Despite having Brains to cushion her fall, it was clear that human bodies were not meant for dropping ten feet onto stone floors.

"Okay, goblin," Bree whispered menacingly, "where are the explosives?" She had already scurried around the lab and found no fireworks. When Brains tried in vain to move his jaw, she rolled her eyes. "Just point, imbecile. I can't believe you're their smartest."

Brains shrugged and shook his head until it was clear that he didn't know where they were. Bree blew a wayward strand of hair out of her face in frustration. "I don't have time to search the halls again—I'm lucky to have made it this far," Bree said. "I'm taking you out of here with me. Without you, there is probably very little chance you furry animals will figure out how the explosives work anytime soon. Besides, I'll need you to point me the way out. And if you lead me down the wrong path, I'll not hesitate to spring you a leak." She showed him the knife, then hoisted him up and set him walking toward the door. "A road less traveled, if you please," she said.

50
NOT BAD FOR A COUPLE OF LOSERS

Just outside of Argh, Sam and PJ found refuge in a small cave. Cheep stood at the cave entrance like a huge guard dog with antennae, while Sam handed PJ the map he'd found in Brains's lab. It showed a tunnel leading away from Argh just beyond their small cave.

PJ studied the map, then cocked his head and stared at Sam for a moment. "After all that's happened," he said, "I gotta ask you why you came down here."

Sam cast his eyes downward, ashamed. "Sorry," Sam said, "I, uh, guess I wanted to see if I had the heart of a warrior, or if I was just a kid who was gonna hold up the Stop-n-Sip someday. Pretty dumb, huh?"

"Oh, man," PJ said. But his expression wasn't one of anger. In fact, he looked guilty. "Hey, kid, you just escaped the nastiest place under earth with just a slacker, an oversized fraidy-bug, and your wits. If that ain't heart, I don't know what is."

Sam's face brightened. "Why'd you come after me?" he asked.

"I checked you outta the jail," PJ said, "and that sorta makes you my, umm, responsibility." He grinned. "And I think they charge a late fee if I don't get you back on time."

Sam smiled back. "Hey, I outsmarted the goblin that tried to eat me on the way here."

"Really?" PJ said.

"Yeah, and I tricked these man-eating cooks into setting me free. And I made friends with Cheep. And when we rode down the wall, that was so cool!"

PJ nodded and listened, but after a moment, he took Sam carefully by the shoulders. "Listen, Sam, I know things all seem like a big adventure now that we're on our way out, but there's some serious stuff still goin' down here. Those people from animal control . . . they're actually guardian soldiers trying to keep the goblins from coming upstairs. There are more of them, but an army of goblins is probably going to wipe them out at the wall, so we can't go back that way. These guardians keep trying to tell me it's my duty, or destiny, or something to come back and fight with them, but now I don't need to." PJ waved the map. "There's a way out."

"So what are you gonna do?" Sam said, staring up at PJ.

"What do you mean, what am I gonna do? I'm taking you out the safe way. It's not like there's any choice."

"You always have a choice," Sam said. "Your dad says so every time I get in trouble."

PJ shook his head, prepared to argue with anything his dad might have said, but then he hesitated. "You know something?" he whispered, half to himself. "That's what Tracker said too. . . ."

51
EWW-YUK TAKES CONTROL

Eww-yuk strode down the hall, pleased with the way he'd handled Slurp and the human in one fell swoop and un-aware that anything was amiss in the city of Argh—until he came across a goblin sentry with its arms wrapped around a stone pillar.

Eww-yuk stared, puzzled. "What are you doing?" he demanded. "This is not your post."

"Muh-mphh-muh-mff-muh," said the sentry.

"Speak up, soldier!"

The goblin turned its head. Its long tongue was tied in a tidy knot up around its ear.

Eww-yuk quickly backtracked to the sentry's post out-side the Great Goblin's hall. He cracked the massive door to the throne room and peeked inside. "Great one?" he whispered. There was no answer.

Eww-yuk stepped into the cavern, eyes darting left and right. He worked his way down the main aisle, past the tow-ering stalagmite pillars. He was halfway to the throne when he stopped in his tracks. "Argh . . . ?"

On the dais at the foot of the throne, the deflated body of the Great Goblin lay beside the body of Tracker.

"Ar-ar-argh." Eww-yuk nodded. "Someone's done me a favor here."

Suddenly, the lookout that had captured PJ outside the city burst into the hall. "I remembered!" the goblin shouted. "I remembered what I was going to tell you!"

"That there are other humans in the city?" Eww-yuk sneered. "Was that it?"

"Yes, but how did you—" The lookout saw the bodies of the Great Goblin and Tracker. It shifted nervously, wringing its paws. "Your father, the Great Goblin, he's . . ."

"Dead." Eww-yuk grinned.

"He has been our leader longer than any of us has lived," the lookout groaned sadly. "You know what this means."

"Yes." Eww-yuk clapped, delighted. "It means at last I am Great Goblin!" He reached down and greedily wrenched the scepter from his father's hand. "Now to deal with that mongrel, Slurp."

Eww-yuk walked through Argh, twirling the scepter and chuckling to himself until he arrived at the empty cave where Slurp and PJ no longer hung. The door stood open, and their chains were broken and empty. He bellowed until the three large guards responsible for his prisoners hustled down the hall toward him.

"Arrrrrrrrgh!" Eww-yuk turned. "Guards! Where is Slurp? Where is the human? Where is the other, smaller human from the meat room?"

He was greeted with three blank looks. "And where were you?" he snapped. The guards looked sheepish. Eww-yuk pointed at them, furious. "Execute each other!" he snapped, then he stormed off.

The guards all raised their weapons, then looked at one another, shrugged, and slipped away.

Eww-yuk set the alarm bell ringing again and stomped down the hall toward the armory, where his goblins were supposed to gather. "Argh! Where are my soldiers? Where are they?"

Along the way, the general kicked open the door to the barracks cavern, expecting to roust a few goblins resting inside.

Boom!

Instead, a huge crowd of fascinated soldiers was gathered in a corner, ignoring the clanging bell they assumed was just another of Eww-yuk's false alarms. Goblins at the back of the crowd looked up and saw the general. They quickly parted to reveal Snivell the chef dealing Texas Hold'em poker to five other goblins like a machine gun.

"Looking for twos, aces, and one-eyed faces," Snivell barked to the players as he flung cards.

"Argh!" complained Blug, and he threw his cards in. "I fold up."

Guh-wat grinned and poured his entire bowl of beetles into a huge pot of writhing bugs in the middle of the table. The other players froze midbet as Eww-yuk stepped to the table, glaring.

Guh-wat looked up at Eww-yuk. "Can we play out this hand?" he said. "I'm all-in."

"Arrrrrrgh!" Eww-yuk howled.

52
THE GUARDIANS' LAST STAND

Unable to wait any longer for Bree, Tracker, or Toady, Braun had led the young guardians back to the same fields they'd fled when the wall had been overrun by the goblins. Returning to their lost fortress had revived difficult emotions in them, for they knew they would face death at the very site that their elders had sacrificed themselves to save their young lives.

They'd tried to sneak up to the wall, but the goblins had spotted them before they could grab the hanging rope ladders, and the beasts had quickly pulled the ropes up out of reach. Now the young guardians huddled among the rocks at the foot of the towering fortress wall as crooked arrows and melon-sized rocks rained down upon them.

"Braun," yelled a wide-eyed young guardian, "what do we do?"

Braun looked pained. He'd led them there, and now they were trapped. He didn't know what to do. He heard his soldiers murmuring and imagined that they must be voicing their discontent with him as their leader. They began gesturing out into the massive cavern. Perhaps in the direction that they planned to flee when they deserted him, he thought.

Braun followed their fingers with sad eyes. But they did not run. Instead, they were pointing at a figure that had appeared across the plains and was stumbling toward them.

Braun's heart leapt. It was Bree.

Bree ran with Brains bound and gagged and strapped across her back. She came on at a dead sprint. The guardians cheered.

But their cheers didn't last long. As Bree neared, their voices quieted, for she ran not only to join them, but also to flee ten goblins that were running right behind her . . . and gaining.

Her guardian friends held their breath, and for a moment it seemed that she might make it to their position out of sheer determination and will. But even she was not immune to fatigue. As she ran, one of her tired strides caught a stone. She stumbled and fell.

Brains tumbled from Bree's back, and the ten goblins were upon her. It was Slurp and nine others. Bree rolled over, fumbling for her sword. Slurp and Drule scooped up Brains and kept running, ignoring her. Bree rose to one knee, taking futile swipes at passing goblins. Inexplicably, none of them stopped to finish her off.

"Come back and fight!" she cried.

They didn't. Instead, they rushed Brains toward the wall, with the other guardians still scattered among the rocks in their path. Arrows and stones stopped falling as Slurp and his contingent approached, and the guardians braced themselves to fight.

But the goblins ran past them too. Befuddled, the guardians watched Slurp and his soldiers romp up to the wall, where they scurried up rope ladders that suddenly dropped down for them.

Bree rose and scrambled to the guardian position among the rocks, where Braun met her. "You're alive!"

"What just happened?" she barked.

"I don't know," he said.

"That was Slurp," Bree said. "He's no coward. He won't hide and toss rocks at us. He'll rally his soldiers, and they'll climb down the wall to wipe us out for good."

"After we're gone, they'll discover the tunnel to the surface," Braun said, stone-faced.

"We are but the first casualties in a worldwide war, Braun," Bree said. She checked the sharpness of her blade's edge and cinched her leather jerkin tight, ready for battle. "Die proud."

"What about Tracker?" Braun asked.

Bree shook her head. "Lost."

"And young Toady?"

"Perhaps he will survive to carry on," she said.

53
A STICKY SITUATION

Meanwhile, Sam and PJ plunged back into the bug tunnel, following Cheep. The giant insect was larger than anything PJ had seen in the tunnel. If Tracker was right about smaller bugs respecting bigger bugs in the insect world, as PJ and Sam hoped, they might be able to run through in Cheep's wake without suffering a horrible, skittering, slimy death.

They were halfway through when Sam saw PJ's flashlight beam swing across something very unbuglike—a pair of leather boots sticking out of a nasty, dripping tangle of goop in one of the larger bug holes.

"Stop," Sam barked, pausing to investigate.

"Stop, my butt," PJ snapped. "This place crawls."

But Cheep stopped with Sam, and PJ had no choice. He didn't want to go any farther without the big bug in the lead.

"Dude," PJ said, frowning, "this is not a good spot to take a break."

"Look at this!" Sam pointed at the boots.

PJ shined his light on them. They were smallish and of guardian make. "It's Toady!" PJ gasped. "Sam, grab a leg!" The boys each grabbed an ankle and yanked. Toady's limp body slid loose from the insect muck with a sickening *shlup-*

ping sound. Suddenly, something inside the hole pulled in the other direction so that Toady was jerked back and forth between the boys and the bug hole like a rope in a tug-of-war.

"Cheep," Sam barked, "help us!"

Cheep leaned down to peer into the bug hole. The massive insect chirped, and whatever had hold of the other end of Toady released him.

Toady flopped out onto the tunnel floor. PJ pulled the young messenger to him, frantic, feeling for a pulse and listening for breaths.

"Who is he?" Sam asked.

"A guardian," PJ said. "Our messenger."

"Is he alive?"

"He's breathing." PJ sighed, relieved.

Sam looked back at the hole. "It made him part of its nest," he said. "I saw another bug do the same thing in the goblin city." Sam shuddered at the memory of the spleech. "Lucky we had Cheep along," he said, patting the giant bug.

"Yeah," PJ said, lifting Toady up onto Cheep's back, "it was almost like your big buddy *ordered* the bug in the hole to let go."

As Sam helped push Toady up, he cocked his head. "Wait," he said, "that gives me a crazy idea."

54
THE BATTLE FOR UNDEREARTH

Bree crouched with Braun as the goblins descended the wall on the rope ladders, just as she had predicted. She took a deep breath as Slurp and his fifty soldiers gathered and marched toward them, weapons drawn. The guardians stood ready behind her, but Slurp's goblins strode to within a few feet of them without shooting a single arrow. One nervous young guardian raised her bow.

Bree stayed her hand and stepped forward. "If you will kill us, then have done with it!" she announced. "We are ready to die."

But Slurp looked beyond Bree. Bree risked a glance back, and, one by one, all the guardians looked past her across the underground plains, where another mass of goblins tromped across the great cavern toward them.

Eww-yuk's army was hundreds of goblins strong, column after column of snarling, furry, club- and spear-wielding soldiers. They moved as a mob, with no discernible order to their ranks. The soldiers waved their stone weapons so wildly that it seemed a miracle they did not brain one another during their trundling march.

Eww-yuk seemed to delight in their raw aggression and lack of organization. He drove them with snarls and growls from his position in the rear, motioning to large guards on the periphery each time a soldier wandered too far from the group. The wandering soldier would receive a quick, firm cuff alongside its ear and quickly plunge back into the pack, more agitated than before.

Archers were mixed among the throng, and on his order the first wave of their arrows took flight, crossing the cave in zigzag paths and hitting just short of the guardians' position.

Slurp strode forward to meet his enemy. He stepped from his ranks, bold and alone. Eww-yuk's archers paused in the face of his bravery.

"Hold!" Slurp boomed, his deep voice rolling across the cavern. "I challenge General Eww-yuk to single combat. Our soldiers need not fight each other."

Even though he stood behind row after ragged row of his own goblins, Eww-yuk looked worried. Some of his soldiers looked back at him, waiting for him to step up and show some courage. He didn't. Instead, he barked at his archers. "Loose!"

Another wave of arrows flew. Slurp winced as he was struck in the gut with a crooked shaft, but he did not falter or retreat. With a mighty roar, he pulled the arrow out and plugged the ooze-spurting hole with a piece of leather that he tore from his own jerkin with his tusks.

"So, General, that is your answer to my challenge, eh?" he called out.

Eww-yuk frowned—he did not have an answer. Slurp

yanked his sword from its sheath. "Then you are every bit the goblin I thought you weren't!"

Slurp held his paw up to signal his own soldiers. He stomped his foot twice, then clapped once. They responded as one, imitating him perfectly—two stomps in quick succession, followed by a synchronized fifty-goblin clap. *Boom-boom-bah!*

Slurp started toward Eww-yuk's army, walking ahead of his own goblins, stomping and clapping. They marched forward behind him and took up his cadence. *Boom-boom-bah! Boom-boom-bah!* They advanced on the opposing force, calm and determined. The stone floor shook, and their pounding rhythm echoed through the cavern.

Eww-yuk's goblins, though vastly more numerous, fidgeted and glanced at one another, unnerved.

Boom-boom-bah! Boom-boom-bah! Slurp's force bore down on the nervous, murmuring lot ahead of them, drawing their weapons and clapping them against their paws and shields as they came.

Slurp hummed, and his soldiers imitated him, humming loudly as they gathered speed. When their raw tune filled the cavern, Slurp roared and ran at his foes. His loyal goblins raised their stone weapons, charging forward behind him, and the fight was on.

The armies came together with a chorus of hacking and crunching sounds as stone weapons connected with goblin flesh and shields. Eww-yuk's loose, fidgeting vanguard buckled under Slurp's organized wave of goblins, whose synchronized line of rising and falling axes and swords tore into them like a grinding machine. Only the larger force's great numbers kept the battle from becoming an instant rout.

Eww-yuk directed traffic from the rear frantically, while the battle-hardened Slurp waded into the heart of the action, tossing smaller goblins left and right in an effort to reach the general. Slurp's soldiers fought madly for their brave captain, carving out a circle around him and pushing forward in a coordinated manner that seemed strangely ungoblin in its symmetry—indeed, it was something Slurp had seen the humans do, and he'd quickly adopted the technique.

The frenzy of battle made Eww-yuk's soldiers forget their kinship with their enemy, and goblin fell against goblin, despite that they knew one another and, in many cases, were related. Even the goblin brothers Nargle and Bargle fought on opposite sides, wrestling and bonking each other with their clubs.

Meanwhile, Bree and her guardians took defensive positions among the rocks, fending off a rush of Eww-yuk goblins with their flashing swords. The cover of the rocks kept Eww-yuk's goblins from surrounding individual humans, and each person was able to defend against just one or two goblins at a time instead of the whole furry mass at once.

Braun found a niche between two rocks where he could keep his back to the stone while he used his great strength to beat down the blows of two club-wielding goblins and

GOBLINS!

buffet them with the heavy hilt of his sword. Bree slid from rock to rock, never showing herself for more than a moment before lashing out to stick surprised goblins with the point of her rapier. Other guardians received similar help from the landscape. They melted away into the rocks and reappeared like magic, their gray cloaks making them difficult to see against the friendly stone. More than once, several goblins chased a single guardian into a forest of stalagmites only to arrive at a dead end and suddenly find a sword at their backs.

But there were still too many. Despite their initial success, Slurp's group, as well as the guardians, were soon forced back to the wall and cornered together. Wave after wave of Eww-yuk goblins fell against Slurp's lines, wearing them down, thinning them out, and eventually regaining the advantage.

Slurp saw the tide turn. With his soldiers losing ground, he climbed atop a rock and raised a tremendous yell at the middle of the writhing pack. "Arrrrrrgh! Eww-yuk!"

The action stopped as though someone had called time-out, and everyone turned toward Slurp. Even Eww-yuk peeked from behind one of his largest guards at the rear of his pack. Slurp pointed to the general. "I will submit to execution if you let my last few soldiers live."

Eww-yuk grinned, smelling victory. "Oh . . . nuh-nuh-nuh-no," he cried with savage glee. "These miserable goblins are no better than the humans they fight alongside." He screeched at his soldiers, "Kill them all!"

Slurp's soldiers and Bree's guardians instinctively

closed ranks, preparing to fight together shoulder to shoulder, and when both groups had braced for Eww-yuk's final assault, Bree found herself standing beside Slurp. He glanced over at her. "Any last thing to say, human?" he asked.

Bree looked the huge goblin up and down. "You smell funny," she replied.

"Thank you." Slurp grinned. "You too."

At the rear of his own army, Eww-yuk raised his sword to give the final order.

"Charrrrrrrge!"

But the cry that echoed across the vast cavern was not Eww-yuk's.

55
FIREWORKS

A plague of huge bugs tore into the left flank of Eww-yuk's army, thousands of insects of all shapes and sizes. At the head of the crawling mass, Sam rode into battle atop Cheep, while PJ and Toady sat astride two fifteen-foot-long grasshopperlike insects. Cheep charged headlong through the field, leading the pack, emboldened by the company of so many of his own kind.

PJ was shirtless and carried a long stick of woodrock with his ANARCHY shirt waving from it like a flag. He bonked goblins with the pole from his mount. "Charrrrge!" he yelled again.

"Wa-hoooooo!" Sam shouted as he waved a goblin dagger from atop Cheep, whose massive tail cleared a path, sweeping furry soldiers head over heels.

Toady swung a large sock full of rocks, bashing goblins as his insect hopped through the fray in great bounds.

The insect army flowed over Eww-yuk's soldiers like a wave, biting, stinging, sliming, and trampling. His goblins turned to swing their pikes and partisans wildly at the cloud of bugs. But for every bug the goblins struck, ten more poured past their weapons to settle on goblin fur and go to their nasty work. Goblins began rolling to the ground, slapping their own limbs and tearing at their own pelts. Their surprised general ducked, dodged, and glanced about frantically with a wide-open mouth—until a bug flew in it.

Among the boulders near the wall, beyond the bug assault, PJ saw a group of Eww-yuk's goblins rush Bree and throw her to the ground. PJ turned his bug to leap up into the rocks with its powerful hind legs. The goblins raised their weapons to strike, but they were so focused on Bree that they didn't see PJ and his massive mount coming. The bug landed on two goblin soldiers at the rear of the group, squashing them like overripe tomatoes, and buffeted the others out of the way.

PJ leaned down to haul Bree up onto the bug with one arm. Bree snatched his hand and swung atop the insect, out of danger. Their eyes met.

"You saved me," she panted.

"Nah." PJ shrugged. "You totally had them where you wanted them." He directed his bug up against the base of the wall, clear of the battle. "But I think you ought to sit out for a bit."

"Thank you," she said, catching her breath, then suddenly she bolted, ran the length of the bug, and hurled herself from its tail back into the fray.

"Dang it!" PJ exclaimed. "I save someone, and they can't even stay saved."

Moments later, Sam pulled Cheep up beside PJ at the wall. PJ turned and eyed the climbing ropes that hung unattended above them. On the battlefield nearby, their friends were still losing. Eww-yuk had too many soldiers, too many weapons. Even the insects weren't enough.

"You gotta climb the wall," PJ told Sam. "Right now nobody will notice if you slip away. Pull the ropes up behind you and go back up the tunnel to the surface."

"What about you?" Sam said.

"They need me here."

Sam stared. The older boy was somehow different than when Sam had met him earlier that day. Sam had thought PJ was cool then—a smart-alec maybe, but cool. Now he knew he was right, only for very different reasons.

Sam nodded and held out his hand. PJ shook it. "It's my destiny, right?" PJ smirked.

"You're not a loser, PJ," Sam said.

"Tell it to my dad," PJ said, then he took a deep breath and spurred his bug, beating a path back into the middle of the fight beside Slurp.

The huge goblin grinned as his human friend joined him, flinging one of Eww-yuk's smaller goblins through the air by the leg. The remaining guardians saw PJ's anarchy banner fly past them and redoubled their efforts. They raised their shields, lowered their shoulders, and pushed forward, driving a human wedge after him through the snarling pack.

Time to go, Sam thought. If he didn't leave now, PJ's sacrifice would be in vain. He turned Cheep toward the wall.

But Sam didn't go. He wanted to help. He wanted to have the heart of a warrior. But what could one twelve-year-old delinquent do? He yanked off the backpack full of fireworks, wishing he'd never seen them, wanting to rid himself of the stolen things, the guilt, and—

Suddenly, a smile crept across his face. He felt his left pants pocket where his cards had been and found the thing he needed still nestled there.

Sam turned Cheep back toward the battle below and gave his bug a firm whack on the abdomen. They galloped down the hill, Sam's mighty insect gaining speed, and when they hit the battlefield, Cheep plowed through the milling goblins and charged to the center of the fray. Sam ducked a flying spear and leapt to his feet atop Cheep's back, climbing to the bug's head, high above the carnage, where he stood tall, at least as tall as a twelve-year-old could be expected to stand.

PJ saw Sam from atop his weary insect nearby. "I told you to go!" he screamed. He looked defeated—his great deed, the best nonslacker thing he'd done in his life, had refused to cooperate.

Sam winced. He hated defying PJ after all the older boy had risked for him, but he set his jaw, determined, and reached into his pocket to grab the butane cigarette lighter he wasn't supposed to have. He raised it in the air like a fan at a rock concert, flicked up a small flame, and held the backpack up beside it.

"Arrrrrrgh!" Sam yelled at the top of his young lungs.

Humans and goblins alike turned to stare as Sam pushed the lit lighter into the pack of fireworks and hurled the pack in the air. For a moment nothing happened, and

Sam held his breath. Then the pack jerked, shuddered, and . . .

BOOM!

The cavern lit up suddenly with blinding orange light. Goblins threw themselves to the ground, shading their eyes. Bugs froze, and humans gazed in awe.

BOOM-BOOM-BOOM!

Fire erupted from the pack in great founts, each new detonation tearing another hole in its shabby leather. Rockets zoomed out in all directions, tracing orange trails across the cave.

BOOM-BOOM-BOOM-BOOM-BOOM!

Some goblins crawled for cover, while explosions went off all around them. Others tried to roll up to imitate rocks. The cavern was drenched in reds, blues, silvers, and flashes of blinding white light until it was fully illuminated and beautiful beyond belief.

BOOM-BOOM-BOOM!

Eww-yuk's goblins were a carpet of cowering fur, all scrambling for holes to crawl into.

"Yes!" Sam shouted.

Nearby, PJ smiled hugely. "Behold!" he yelled with glee to the crowd. "Behold and bow before the new guardian warriors!"

Bree's guardians cheered and once again charged through the sniveling goblins. Slurp grinned, rousting his own dazed soldiers. His goblins rose and threw themselves at Eww-yuk's confused troops. Panicked bugs skittered through them all. Eww-yuk's forces broke ranks and fled, and none ran faster than the general himself. As he ran, Eww-yuk yelled commands over his shoulder. "Don't flee! Stand your ground!"

Suddenly, it was over. Bree and her remaining guardians stood panting alongside Slurp's goblins as the bug swarm moved off across the cavern, fleeing the rocket blasts along with Eww-yuk's scattered troops.

Sam stood at the center of the victory atop Cheep's head—the best seat in the house to the best fireworks show he'd ever seen.

As their common enemy retreated, Bree took stock of Slurp's goblins. They were as beaten and tired as her own soldiers. She tossed her weapon down and bid her guardians to do the same. They looked at her with raised eyebrows, but did it. The goblins studied their human allies carefully, then, one by one, they imitated them, dropping their own weapons.

PJ looked around. "Hey, where's my man Slurp?"

56
A GOBLIN FAMILY REUNION

Eww-yuk stood at the edge of the swamp just past the carnivorous grass field, unwilling to risk wading in. He'd broken off from the larger group when the harassing bugs followed them. He didn't know he was being followed until he heard the whisper of a sword being pulled from its sheath.

Eww-yuk turned and snarled. It was Slurp. Eww-yuk raised his own clean, unused sword. His armor bore no sign of struggle. In contrast, Slurp's sword was battered and notched, and his torn leather armor hung from him like a well-loved shirt, complete with tattered holes.

"Argh!" warned Eww-yuk. "Stop there, Captain. I order you to put down your weapon."

"Call me brother . . . brother," Slurp said. He moved toward Eww-yuk, calm and confident.

"I don't see you putting down your weapon, *half* brother." Eww-yuk frowned.

"Never give up your weapon," Slurp said. "Old Slouch taught me that when I was just a pup. You remember being a pup, eh? When we had other brothers?"

"I am the only goblin that matters," Eww-yuk barked. "Me!"

"Arggh! You would have killed me like you murdered the rest." Slurp came on without further words and let his weapon speak for him. He aimed a powerful blow at Eww-yuk's head, just missing and driving the general backward into the swamp.

Eww-yuk whipped his sword in a descending arc, the way he'd been taught in the confines of the training room. Slurp dodged easily and kicked a small stone at Eww-yuk, a trick he'd learned in the wild caverns. Eww-yuk was distracted and ducked, giving Slurp the chance to leap in and rain a series of blows down upon him. Eww-yuk parried only twice before Slurp struck his furry forearm hard with the pommel of his sword and Eww-yuk's own gleaming weapon fell into the mud and sank. Slurp's worn blade nestled itself up against the general's thick neck.

Eww-yuk tensed as Slurp drew nose to nose with him and spoke in a low growl. "I will stop you from ever making our own soldiers fight our other own soldiers again. And when I tell the Great Goblin, he will make you not a general anymore."

Then Eww-yuk smiled an unpleasant smile. "Ah . . . my poorly spoken brother, but you don't understand. You never were very smart, were you?"

Slurp hesitated. It was true that he often did not understand things. "I understand enough," he said.

"Then do you understand why I am Great Goblin now?" Eww-yuk pulled the scepter from beneath his cloak.

Slurp's sword went limp in his hand. "Our father, he's . . . ?"

"Dead," snapped Eww-yuk. "Yes, yes, gone, dried up, shriveled away."

Slurp slumped, devastated. His sword point dragged on the ground. Eww-yuk saw his chance and struck a surprise blow with the scepter.

Clang! Slurp's sword flew out of his hand.

"So loyal, yet so dumb," Eww-yuk spat, pawing the scepter eagerly, "the whole slobbering lot of you from that second litter."

Slurp glanced down. A slime trail ran through the muck. Defenseless, he edged backward along it, leading Eww-yuk into the swamp. "I might not be smart . . . ," Slurp said.

"You're not," Eww-yuk agreed.

"And I might not be first litter," Slurp continued, wading deeper into the muck and mire. "But as a leader, I serve my goblins, not they serve me." He kicked through muck, purposefully splashing to the edge of a large sinkhole.

"That is why you are not Great Goblin and I am!" Eww-yuk raised the scepter for the killing stroke. "And now, as the new Great Goblin, I order you to die. . . ."

But at the height of his swing, Eww-yuk paused. He turned as a shadowy form rose from the swamp, dripping mud and slime. Its blunt antenna jerked his direction, and it made a great sucking sound as it surged up out of the sinkhole to tower over him. Eww-yuk tried to shrink away as the giant sweeper slithered forward, searching for the source of the splashing.

The general whined pitifully and thrust the scepter up into the belly of the beast. The ornate rod sizzled and melted. Behind him, Slurp stepped forward and gave Eww-yuk a soft push in the back. Eww-yuk teetered at the edge of the sinkhole, then lost his balance and fell into the slug.

Schlopp! The general stuck to the vertical underside of the sweeper. His expression was a mixture of surprise and regret as he began to dissolve before Slurp's eyes, melting into black, oozy goblin jelly.

Slurp watched the grim end of his half brother for a time, then picked up the melted scepter and turned to walk away. A few steps later he heard a sound. He glanced at a nearby bog, curious and wary. "Who's there?" he called.

57
LICKING WOUNDS

Bree and her company retreated behind the wall, lifting their injured to safety in makeshift baskets with long ropes. Slurp's injured goblins were brought over the wall too. They patched oozing leaks in their hides, using their long tongues to clean their wounds.

Sam found Brains in a storage bunker, still bound and gagged. The female archer that Slurp's goblins had captured earlier that day was also imprisoned there. Sam pulled his dagger and quickly relieved them both of their bonds.

Just then, a furry figure pulled itself up one of the rope ladders onto a battlement. Everyone looked as Slurp climbed—torn, battered, and with a hole in his gut—over the top of the wall carrying a large, muddy object on his wide shoulder. "Human!" he called.

"I think he means me," PJ said. He stood and walked up onto the scaffolding to meet the goblin captain.

"I found this in the swamp," Slurp said. He dumped his burden on the scaffolding. *Whump!* It was a mud-caked human in rough shape. "I think it still lives."

Bree jumped to her feet and shrieked, "Whitey!" She rushed up the scaffolding and knelt down.

Slug-acid burns and mud covered Whitey's entire body, but he was able to open his eyes. "I dreamed that a goblin . . . helped me," he wheezed. "This must be the sweet afterlife." He tried to sit up.

"Lie down," said Bree. "You're at the wall, and we've led our forces to victory."

"You? My little sister?"

"No," Bree said, "not just your little sister. I am the leader of the guardians—your leader, until you recover. Now lie down."

Slurp looked over at PJ. "My main man," the huge captain said, "you told me that I could do it, and look . . . now I am Great Goblin." Slurp held up the handle of the melted scepter.

"Yeah?" PJ smirked. "What's so great about you?"

Slurp stared for a moment, then began to laugh loud and long.

58
A BRIGHTER FUTURE

The guardians watched Slurp and his soldiers march across the cavern, away from the wall, then the humans pulled the ropes up behind the goblins, locking them out.

"You gave him Brains," Bree complained to PJ.

"Eh, he needs 'im," PJ replied.

"Besides," Sam added, "he let us keep that archer woman and this cool fortress. Fair trade, I say."

"It's a treaty, then?" asked Braun.

"No." Bree frowned. "He wouldn't promise not to come back and attack us."

"That's 'cuz he knows his promise wouldn't mean anything," PJ said. "Apparently, we taught them to be big, fat liars."

Slurp led his soldiers home across the underground plain.

"I still say we should have ate them," Drule complained to Slurp.

"And the gadgets!" whined Brains. "We've lost the gaaaaadgets!"

Brains and Drule were not the only goblins to find it odd that Slurp had made a deal with the humans. It was strange to treat food as though it was their equal and to bargain with it. Other goblins joined in the rising murmurs of discontent.

"Arrrgh!" Slurp whirled and shined a bright beam in their faces. The soldiers gasped and cringed, covering their eyes. It was as if their leader had magically cast a blinding light from his paw. The grumbling ceased abruptly.

Slurp held the police-issue flashlight in his hand and grinned. After a moment, he slipped the flashlight back into his cloak, clicked it off, and walked on, completely in command. "The illuminator," PJ had called it, "a useful tool, even though it doesn't kill or cook anyone." He was right, thought Slurp. The gadget got the attention of his soldiers without harming them in the least.

Slurp hummed as he walked. It was a new day for goblins. They had a new leader, and he had some new ideas thanks to the two strange humans with boing on their feet and songs in their hearts. The illuminator was only the beginning.

59
GOOD-BYE

The guardians chattered about gathering supplies and re-shaping the battlements to repel grappling hooks as they began to put things back in order at the wall.

Sam found PJ. "Hey, PJ . . . I'm, uh, hungry."

"Me too, kid," PJ said.

Bree clapped Sam on the shoulder. "The boy swings a good sword."

PJ stepped to Sam and gently pulled him away from Bree. "Yeah, he's totally got the heart of a warrior and all, but this ain't exactly a nurturing environment down here." PJ looked down at Sam. "I never realized that protecting mankind and looking after a kid at the same time would be so hard."

Sam beamed. "It's even harder looking after a teen-ager," he smirked.

PJ laughed. "I gotta get him back home," he said to Bree.

"By the way," Sam said, pulling out the caver map and tossing it to Bree, "somebody's discovered another tunnel down from the surface, which you guys will probably wanna check out and block off."

Moments later, PJ and Sam were mounting Cheep.

Bree followed them, searching for words. "I was, ummm, wrong about you," she said to PJ. "Tracker was right. You were a brave soldier sent to help us."

"Nah," PJ said, shaking his head. "Tracker had some crazy ideas. He also thought the ghost of his long-lost brother, Hunter, sent me here. But *you* were right—I'm no soldier. I'm just a kid from L.A. that wandered down here by accident." Sam spurred Cheep, and they started up the slope.

"The bravery in your blood cannot be disclaimed," Bree called after him. "Risking your life to save me was no accident, eh?"

PJ turned to wave a last farewell. "Okay, you got me." He winked. "*That* . . . I meant to do."

"Bye-bye!" Sam yelled as Cheep headed up the hill toward the hidden tunnel to the surface.

60
DAD

The border sensor's post was buried ten feet into the earth and calibrated to detect any movement beneath the ground. By the time PJ and Sam pushed up the trapdoor in the woods, the alarm had been tripped for several minutes.

The two boys climbed out of the tunnel. The light of the moon seemed as bright as the sun—too bright for Cheep's bulbous eyes. The giant insect gazed after Sam for a long moment, then reluctantly slipped back into the dimness of the tunnel, seeming to know that it didn't belong in the surface world.

The air topside smelled clean and plentiful, and the boys drank it in with greedy gulps as they limped past the sensor post, tattered and battered, leaning on each other.

A car crunched to a stop on the path just beyond the trees. Its blue and red lights flashed through the brush.

"Uh-oh," PJ said. "Now the real trouble starts."

Sam could see PJ tense up. It was sad. PJ was a good guy, and his dad was a good guy too, but they were so different. *They need common ground*, Sam thought. "You know," he said, "your dad's really okay. He's always been good to me."

"Maybe *you* should be his son."

"Maybe you should stop thinking up smart-alec comments while he's talking and just listen to what he has to say," Sam replied.

There was a moment of silence, and Sam was surprised when the older boy didn't argue or make another wisecrack.

"I know what he's going to say." PJ frowned. "I just don't know what I'm going to tell him. I really screwed up . . . as usual."

"Try the truth, maybe?" Sam suggested. "Tell him we were busy saving the world."

"Right. What are the odds my dad is gonna believe that?"

The boys broke cover and stepped directly into the path of the patrol car's headlights.

"Percy!" shouted a voice from behind the wall of blinding light.

Sam watched PJ wince and brace himself for the coming lecture. But the lecture didn't come. Instead, Officer Myrmidon burst from the light and gave PJ an enormous bear hug. "I was so worried about you, son," he exclaimed.

PJ looked around, bewildered, his shoulders squished up around his ears from the force of his dad's desperate embrace. "Hi, Dad."

The tall officer released him. "And Sam . . . you're okay too! Thank the good earth."

Sam waved sheepishly. He was glad to be back, but tired. He didn't have the energy to launch into an explanation. "Hi," he said.

PJ's dad took his son by the shoulders. "When I got back, you two were gone. I didn't know where you went, but when the sensor went off, I thought the worst. . . . I just threw my equipment in the car and rushed out here."

After hours in the dark caverns, the bright lights hurt Sam's eyes, so he stepped past the headlights to the side of the cruiser while PJ listened to his father. The trunk lid was open. It seemed their appearance had interrupted Officer Myrmidon, who'd been retrieving something from the back.

For a moment, Sam didn't understand what he saw. He reached in and pulled out a long, beaten sword. It was old, nicked, and dented, but polished as though someone kept it prepared for use. The sword wasn't the only object in the trunk. Sam reached in again.

PJ and his father faced each other. "Dad, I have to tell you . . . I don't have a good explanation for all this."

"I don't think you need one," Sam said, stepping between them. "But maybe your dad does." He held up the sword in one hand and a vest of leather armor in the other.

Officer Myrmidon stared, then took a deep breath. He reached out and gently removed the sword from Sam's grasp.

PJ watched in disbelief as the weapon changed hands. His father handled the blade smoothly, expertly, as comfortable with its heft as if he were born with it in his hand.

"I think I know why you never left Sumas, Officer Myrmidon," Sam said.

"Yes," Officer Myrmidon said, staring at the sword as though its presence was making him talk to his son. "I ran away from my responsibilities when I was about your age, Percival, and I came up here. I'd taken an oath, and I should have gone back down. But I met your mother, we had you, and I couldn't go back. I loved the two of you too much."

Sam was surprised to see the big man's eyes grow damp.

"What are you saying?" PJ asked, his own teenage eyes flitting from the sword to his father's face. He seemed confused and anxious, but eager to understand.

"I had to find a way to stay topside, but fulfill my commitment too. I couldn't leave altogether and go with you to L.A., away from here. I took an oath to guard this place. Commitment, security, and responsibility." He sighed. "It's hard to explain."

"No, it isn't," Sam said. "PJ understands more than you know. Show him . . ."

Officer Myrmidon took stock of Sam, who felt older somehow, as though he had matured a decade since he'd been booked into jail only a half day earlier. PJ's dad nodded to Sam and held up the sword.

The moonlight glinted off the blade so that his son could read the inscription near the hilt, and Sam watched as, in that moment, PJ suddenly understood his father. For the name on his dad's sword was . . . *Hunter*.

CHINOOK MIDDLE SCHOOL
LIBRARY